STITCH HEAD

THE MONSTER HUNTER

For my editor, Jane Harris
The true keeper of Castle Grotteskew
~Guy Bass

For Natasha Mott
~Pete Williamson

Stitch Head

THE MONSTER HUNTER

Guy Bass

Illustrated by Pete Williamson

stripes

Foreword is Forearmed
(An Ominous Ode)

In the darkness, Little Albert spotted Grotteskew,

The castle stood upon a hill; 'twas evil through and through.

So Little Albert climbed the hill to see if it was true

That monsters lurked within its walls

(I wouldn't have — would you?)

What did he spot? What did he see? It seems we'll never know.

For Little Albert vanished, and the town was full of woe.

WELCOME TO
GRUBBERS NUBBIN

(POPULATION 639)

Some considerable while after
Ye Olden Days
In the Early Days of
Yesteryear

STARGAZING
(Nothing but trouble)

Behold! The uncertain pleasure of Grubbers Nubbin at night! With the lamp lights extinguished, it was as dark as bad dreams, bone-achingly cold and, more often than not, almost *too* quiet. Who knew what creatures lurked in the dark? Who could say what pant-wettingly terrifying monstrosities waited in the shadows, eager to rain chaos and terror upon the townsfolk? The horrors! The horrors!

But to be honest, hardly anything ever actually *happened*. It was usually less eventful than a sneeze. The most excitement you could expect was a spot of stargazing.

"What d'you see, Arabella?" asked the old woman, pointing her walking stick to the sky.

"Stars?" replied Arabella. She was an untidy girl of three years old, with an unwashed face and hair like a bird's nest. She glanced down at her brand-new pair of well polished boots. "Kick the stars!"

"Now, now, we don't kick stars, Arabella … but only 'cause we can't reach 'em!" the old woman cackled. She peered up into the sky, her expression suddenly distant and strange. "It's like my own nan used to say — stars are for *gazing* at."

"Gazing's *bore-ding*," groaned Arabella, running in circles and flapping her arms like a bird.

"Yep! Ain't nothin' duller except watching paint dry," agreed Arabella's nan. "But that's 'ow life is — my old nan taught me gazing, now

I'm teachin' you. So let's get started, before we freeze our nostrils off." She waved her stick at the sky. "The idea's to find *consternations* – shapes 'n' such made out o' the stars. See that big bunch up there? That's called the *Old Sock* ... that lot over there's the *Clod of Mud* ... there's the *Half a Turnip*..."

"Mud is boring, turnips is boring, stars is boring," huffed Arabella. "Grubbadubbin is boring."

"Oi! Don't knock *boring*, you mucky rotten goat – life is better when it's boring," chided Arabella's nan. "Right, now you try. What do you see?"

Arabella huffed and then peered up into the sky, squinting to make out shapes. For the longest time the stars just looked like stars. But then, slowly, a shape began to emerge within the distant clusters.

"I see . . . I see . . ." Arabella said. "A *monster!*"

"A *what*? Crusty bloomers! Hush your mouth!" shrieked her nan.

"Monster! Monster! Monster!" cried Arabella, pointing up at the sky. "The sky's full of monsters!"

"Hush, I say!" hissed Arabella's nan. "Where did you get such an imagination? Not from me, that's for certain! No good can come from thinking such thoughts or saying such words!"

"But I *like* monsters," replied Arabella defiantly. Then she thought for a moment and added, "Nan, are monsters real?"

Arabella's nan turned and glanced up to the top of a nearby hill. There loomed Castle Grotteskew. The castle was the home of Mad Professor Erasmus, the maddest mad professor of all. The townsfolk of Grubbers Nubbin lived in constant fear of the castle. Some claimed to have heard roars and screams coming from inside ... others to have seen strange things atop the castle walls ... not-human things. Rumour had it that Professor Erasmus *made* monsters.

But everyone agreed that the castle was to be avoided at all costs.

Everyone except Arabella.

"*Castle Grotty-skoo!*" she squealed, following her nan's gaze up to the castle. "Monsters!"

"Now, you listen to me, Arabella Guff," said Nan, taking Arabella by the shoulders. "Monsters ain't to be liked or to be looked for, not ever. Monsters ain't *nothing but trouble.*"

"But I like trouble, too," said Arabella.

"I'm serious!" snapped her nan. "I want you to promise me, no more talk about monsters. No more even *thinking* about monsters. And certainly no seeing 'em in the blinkin' stars!"

"But—"

"*Promise* me," said Arabella's nan again.

Arabella sighed. "I promise," she grumbled, scuffing the ground with her feet.

"Good girl." Arabella's nan pointed her

stick up into the air. "Now try again, what do you see?"

Arabella looked up at the sky, and shrugged. "*Old sock?*" she said.

"That's more like it!" Her nan breathed a long sigh of relief, as a grin flashed across Arabella's face.

"And *monsters,*" she whispered to herself.

SEVEN YEARS
LATER

LET'S PRETEND WE'RE MONSTERS

(A bit of excitement)

In a castle full of monsters
There's noise from time to time
But for weeks it has been tranquil
Which suits us monsters fine

Signed,
The Creations of Grotteskew

"GRR…"

A great, clawed hand reached around the dungeon door, pushing it open with a rusty *creeeaak*. A monstrous thing of implausible proportions stepped inside. The beastly Creature's three arms stretched out, tail and tentacles writhing, its single glaring eye probing the darkness.

"GRRoOoWRR…" it whispered.

It loomed over a tiny, makeshift bed on the floor, upon which lay an even tinier, almost-human shape, covered from head to toe in a blanket. The Creature bared a mouthful of jagged teeth. It extended its largest, most-clawed arm and dragged the blanket from the bed, with a blood-curdling roar.

"GRRRRRAAAAAAUH!"

The bed was empty but for a pile of rags.

"Boo," whispered Stitch Head, hopping out from behind a crate.

"Eeeeeeeeeeeeee—!" the Creature squealed in surprise. The sound was so high-pitched and shrill that even the tiniest mouse would have considered it feeble. The Creature flung its arms and tentacles in every direction as it dived in horror behind a pile of boxes.

"Don't HURT me, monster!" howled the Creature. "I'm too YOUNG and CREATIVE to die!"

"It's all right, Creature, it's me! It's Stitch Head!" cried Stitch Head.

As the first creation of Mad Professor Erasmus, Stitch Head was also his least monstrous. He was small, slight and barely taller than a toddler, with a patchwork of stitches covering his ashen face.

"Stitch Head? I KNEW that!" the Creature lied, clambering out from behind the boxes and trying to look casual. The Creature was one of the professor's more-recent creations. In stark contrast to Stitch Head, it was a massive, menacingly monstrous mishmash, with three arms, numerous tentacles and a single, cyclopean eye in the centre of its face. But since Stitch Head had cured it of a nasty case of werewolfism, it was as gentle as a kitten's lick.

"NICE idea, making a FAKE you out of RAGS," the Creature added, inspecting the bed. "I NEARLY lost my ICE-cool COMPOSURE…"

"I-I didn't mean to scare you," said Stitch Head. "I learned that trick while I was escaping from my master's last creation. Of course, she *was* trying to pull my arms off…"

"GOOD old ANTOINETTE. How IS she?" the Creature asked.

"Much better for a dose of Psycho Path to Enlightenment potion," said Stitch Head. "She prefers sewing to savagery now."

"GREAT! She can join my KNIT WITS and SEW-AND-SEWS Crochet Club!" boomed the Creature excitedly.

Stitch Head smiled. It made a nice change to have only the odd rampaging creation to worry about. He had spent his almost-life keeping the professor and Castle Grotteskew safe, even though his master had all but forgotten he existed. But after the events of recent months (attempted kidnappings, angry mobs, ghostly hauntings and the castle almost burning down, not to mention an entirely chaotic visit from a hundred human orphans) it finally seemed as though almost-life was returning to normal – or as normal as it could be.

"*There* you are," said a voice. Stitch Head and the Creature turned to see Arabella standing in the doorway. She was a determinedly scruffy girl of nearly eleven, with a thick, tangled mess of bird's-nest hair. Only her polished boots were vaguely presentable. "What are you playing? I'm bored out of my brain!" she added.

"Only the GREATEST game EVER!" declared the Creature. "It's called Let's Pretend We're MONSTERS."

"Let's pretend we're...?" began Arabella. "But you *are* monsters."

"No, but REAL monsters," said the Creature. "MONSTROUS monsters, like the ones the PROFESSOR makes! I mean, before Stitch Head CURES them."

"That sounds like the stupidest idea for a game I ever heard," chuckled Arabella. "Can I play?"

"Of course! IVO is still HIDING around here SOMEWHERE, waiting to TERRIFY our HEADS off," boomed the Creature. "SO, do you want to be a MONSTER or an unsuspecting VICTIM ... or BOTH?"

"Monster! Obviously," Arabella replied.

"You can take my place," said a relieved Stitch Head. He collected his shoulder bag and carefully began filling it with potion bottles. "I should check on the professor's newest creation. It's only a day or so off being awakened…"

"Stitch Head, have you ever thought it might be a bit more exciting if you didn't make all the prof's monsters un-monstrous?" said Arabella. "I mean, it's so blinkin' *boring* around here."

"But – but I *like* boring," said Stitch Head, imagining the havoc his master's creations might cause if he didn't create potions to relieve their rage. He slung the potion bag over his shoulder. "Boring means no one is running for their lives."

"You sound like my ol' nan – she *loved*

boring. Come on, I'll show you," said Arabella. With that, she ducked under the Creature's legs and up the dungeon steps.

"What? Where are we going?" asked Stitch Head, hurrying after her.

"WAIT, what about our GAME?" the Creature called after them. "We STILL haven't FOUND—"

"Boo!"

The oval head of Ivo suddenly popped out from the Creature's coat pocket. Despite his tiny, doll-like stature and cloak of rags, the sight was too much for the Creature to take.

"Eeeeeeeeeeee—!"

THE SUDDEN AND UNEXPECTED APPEARANCE OF A GIANT FLYING EGG

(That must be some chicken)

MAD MUSING No. 44

"I expect to expect the
unexpected, expectantly."

From *The Occasionally Scientific
Writings of Professor Erasmus Erasmus*

Stitch Head followed Arabella up a series of steep, winding staircases until they reached the castle ramparts.

"W-what are we doing out here?" asked Stitch Head, who generally preferred a ceiling over his head to an endless expanse of sky.

"You like boring? Well, stargazing has boring coming out of its ears," said Arabella. "I used to gaze with my ol' nan, back in the day. It's as dull as counting cobbles."

Stitch Head peered upwards. It was a clear spring night and the stars looked as bright as he had ever seen them. "What do I have to do?" he asked.

"Just look up and then pretend like the stars make shapes," replied Arabella. "You see that big blob of 'em over there? That's the *Picked Nose*. And that run of 'em there? That's the *Gob o' Spit*. Now you try…"

"Uh, OK…" said Stitch Head, still confused as to how the "game" worked. He looked up. "I see, uh … the cluster of stars?"

"Cluster of— Stargazing ain't *that* boring!" laughed Arabella. "You have to make somethin' out of nothin'. Go on, have another go…"

Stitch Head stared upwards again, searching for a discernible shape among the constellations. He peered at the stars for what seemed like forever, the wind whistling around the ramparts, the distant sound of his master's mad cackles echoing from deep within the castle.

"Wait, I think I see something," he muttered at last. "I see … an *egg?* A giant … flying … egg?"

"Now you're getting it!" chuckled Arabella.

"No, I mean I can *really* see it," added Stitch Head, pointing upwards. "Look! A giant flying egg!"

Arabella squinted. A huge, white oval shape was soaring through the sky towards them, looming ever larger. It looked for all the world like a giant flying egg.

"Blimey, that must be some chicken!" said Arabella.

"It's – it's coming this way…" muttered Stitch Head.

As the shape drew closer, it became clear that the egg was in fact some sort of oddly shaped balloon made from taut white fabric. Beneath it, suspended by four wires was a strange wooden contraption like a tiny horse cart. Four metal wings protruded from its sides, flapping creakily up and down, down and up, while at its back, propellers whirred noisily, spluttering and spitting. The flying machine banked in the air – left then right – before heading straight towards them.

"It's gonna crash! Move!" Arabella cried, knocking Stitch Head to the ground as the strange object swooped over their heads, grazing the walls of the castle and skimming the ramparts. It bounced and skidded before finally careening into a tower with an almighty…

KROOM!

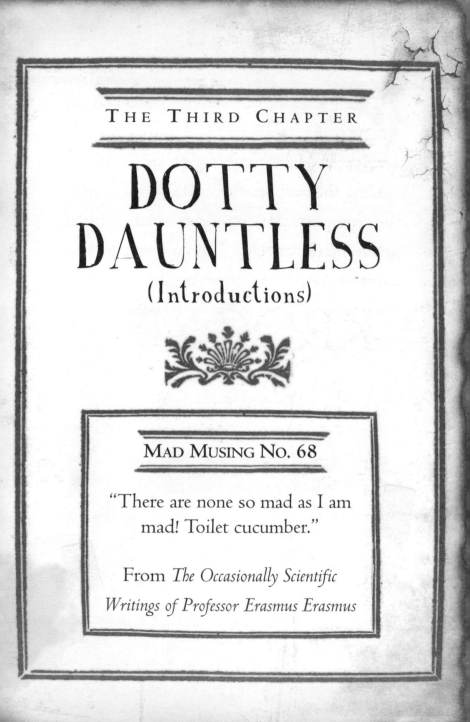

DOTTY DAUNTLESS

(Introductions)

MAD MUSING No. 68

"There are none so mad as I am
mad! Toilet cucumber."

From *The Occasionally Scientific
Writings of Professor Erasmus Erasmus*

"Blimey!" shouted Arabella as the flying machine skidded to an unwieldy halt, plumes of smoke pouring from its engine. "What the blinkin' stink…?"

"Are you all right?" said Stitch Head, scrambling to his feet. "What is that th—"

"Great thunder! The take-offs are a cinch but the landings are rougher than a rhino's rump!"

From inside the flying machine's wooden cockpit emerged a large, muscular figure … a *human*. As she planted her feet firmly on the ramparts, her fists pressed against her hips, Stitch Head saw that she was taller and more broad-shouldered than any human he had ever seen. She was dressed in a leather jacket and khaki trousers. On one hip was a holstered pistol, on the other an impressive hunting knife and she wore a coiled length of rope slung over her shoulder. Upon her head sat a large safari hat, complete with goggles, that went some way to containing her thick, loosely bound bun of bright, silver hair.

"Your mouths are justly agape, for even the curly beaked Andruvean Condor could not have executed such a graceful landing!" said the woman with a wink, her voice as deep as a chasm.

"Graceful? You near killed us, you mucky rotten goat!" shouted Arabella, as Stitch Head ducked behind her. "I ought to kick your nose off!"

"What a marvellously mad moppet!" the woman guffawed, peering admiringly at Arabella. "Why, you remind me of the Leopard Man of Lumbuktah – wild and fierce, with hair that cannot be tamed by brush alone!"

"Eh?" said Arabella, more than a little taken aback.

Stitch Head peered at the strange human. He was gripped with dread. Who was she? What did she want? And more importantly, how soon could he get rid of her? After all, Professor Erasmus had one rule and one rule only: *no visitors*.

"No visitors!" Stitch Head echoed his master's instruction in an urgent whisper to Arabella.

"Keep your stitches on," Arabella replied. "She's just some old biddy. How much trouble can she be?"

"So, do you like my most excellent sky carriage? I built it myself!" boomed the woman obliviously. "They said it couldn't be done, but *they* are full of trumps and humbugs, don't you think? If the mind dares to dream, there is nothing that cannot be achieved! Of course, it also helps if you have oodles of cold, hard cash."

"N-no visitors!" said Stitch Head, this time loud enough for the woman to hear.

"Ah, but like the spotless jaguar, I am the exception that proves the rule!" the woman laughed. "I have been known by many names – the Princess of Persiana, the Queen of Kartumba, the Tigress of Tindin Singh, Dances with a Hat On ... or, quite simply, Lady Dorothea Drucilla Dolores Day-Drummond-Day Dauntless! But you can call me Dotty!"

"Dotty Dauntless?" said Arabella, trying out the name.

"I was born in a thunderstorm with hair upon my head and a quest between my ears!" continued Dotty Dauntless. "I travelled here on a wing and a dream across two oceans and three continents ... over deserts, mountains, jungles and lands untold! I do what I am, and I am what I seek: mystery, discovery, adventure and excitement!"

Excitement! thought Stitch Head in horror. *What happened to boring?*

"And now for you!" continued Dotty, glaring at Arabella. "Do not tell me your name; I shall certainly deduce it, for my mind is as sharp as the spears of the *Unblunta* tribe! From your manner I would say you are not used to waiting, so your name must be early in the alphabet. At the same time, you resent the name for you think it too pretty — *trop belle*, as the French-folk would say. But not Belle, for I am sure even 'B' is too long to wait… Only an 'A' name will do for you, so then your name must surely be — not Annabelle but — Arabella!"

"*Blimey*," said Arabella. She was as speechless as Stitch Head had ever seen her.

"And what's this? Some sort of pet?" continued Dotty Dauntless, pointing at Stitch Head. "I'll bet my lucky hat your name is Scamp. A fine pet's name!"

"Pet? He ain't no pet," said Arabella. "His name is Stitch Head and he's the first creation of the maddest mad professor of all!"

"Arabella...!" Stitch Head cried.

"'Stitch Head'? The name doesn't suit you at all! Still, a bet's a bet," Dotty scoffed. She took off her hat and dropped it on to Arabella's head. Then she inspected Stitch Head closely. "So, you're saying little Scamp is the work of Mad Professor Erasmus? Well, he won't do at all. Great thunder, no!"

"You — you know my master?" Stitch Head asked. Fear gripped him tighter — was Dotty here for the professor?

"I do not — but he is the reason I am here," she said, her eyes flashing with excitement. "Or rather, his *monsters*."

"M-monsters?" repeated Stitch Head.

"But first things first!" cried Dotty, clapping her hands together. "What's for dinner?"

BOOTS AND BETS

(Dinner with Dotty Dauntless)

Dear Madthing Arabellur

Here is a tastey pie, made from the finest pork.

Have a nice dinnur

Yours troothfully,

The Orphuns

(also known as the Little Terrors)

Stitch Head felt his chest tighten as he tried to think of a way to rid the castle of Dotty Dauntless. Dotty, meanwhile, clearly had no intention of leaving.

"An adventurer cannot live on exploits alone!" she cried, taking long, deliberate sniffs of air. "I must *eat*."

"Ain't no one eats nothin' around here except me," said Arabella, adjusting her new, thoroughly oversized safari hat.

"Then you hold the key to my survival, my mad moppet!" replied Dotty. "An empty gut is a feeble mind, and I'm hungrier than the time I was stranded for a month in the Lost Dunes of Mowadeeb with nothing for sustenance but the suspect secretions of sand scorpions. I'll tell you what, let's make a wager. I bet I can find your food before you. If I do, you must share it with me. If not, I shall give you ... my *boots*."

"Boots?" repeated Arabella. She glanced down and her jaw fell open – Dotty Dauntless wore the most impressive pair of boots she had ever seen. Sturdy, rust-brown leather polished to perfection, with burnished steel buckles and toe caps that looked like they could knock down a wall.

They were the boots Arabella kicked with in her dreams.

"*Deal*," she said.

"What?" blurted Stitch Head. "You can't! I mean, you can't go into the castle! The professor doesn't like— My master would never allow— No visitors!"

"Yeah? What about all them orphans you let through the Great Door last month?" tutted Arabella, still staring at Dotty's boots.

"But that was – I mean there was no other – I mean—" Stitch Head began awkwardly.

"Details! A bet is a bet, little Scamp!" interrupted Dotty Dauntless. Then she took another sniff of air and began striding down toward the nearest stairwell into the castle.

"No, wait!" cried Stitch Head, as Dotty disappeared through the door. "We have to—"

"Beat her to my room? Too *right* we do," grinned Arabella, a peculiarly intense look in her eyes. "Let's not take any chances. You know every shortcut and hidden passage in this place, Stitch Head. Get us there, double quick!"

"But – but—" Stitch Head stuttered.

"But nothing!" Arabella shrieked, grabbing Stitch Head by the shoulders. "I need them boots!"

+‑+‑++‑+‑+‑++‑+‑+‑+‑+‑+‑++‑+‑+‑+‑++‑+‑+‑+

Stitch Head reluctantly led Arabella through a maze of secret doors and concealed ink-black passageways — passageways he had spent an almost-lifetime memorizing (and had often used to escape his master's mad monsters). Before long they emerged from behind a tattered curtain into the familiar main hall. At the far end of the hall was a corridor leading to a wooden door. Upon it were written the words:

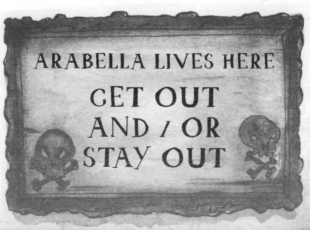

ARABELLA LIVES HERE
GET OUT
AND / OR
STAY OUT

"Nice one, Stitch Head! Them boots are mine!" Arabella cried. She pressed her hat on to her head and made a dash for the door…

But it was already open.

"Come in, come in!" said a voice. "You're just in time to be slightly too late."

Arabella and Stitch Head skidded to a horrified halt. Lying on Arabella's bed, holding a plate piled high with pies, fruit and bread, was Dotty Dauntless. Arabella's pet monkey-bat Pox (half-monkey, half-bat, generally savage) was flitting around the room, barking and snarling at the intruder.

"GruKK! YaBBit!"

"Turns out there's plenty of grub to go round!" Dotty continued, tossing a piece of pie into her mouth. "Help yourself!"

"How did you know where to find my stash?" growled Arabella.

"I sniffed it out, of course," explained Dotty Dauntless. "I spent more than a year learning *Pong-fu* with the blindfolded monks of Lobandanna. They rely purely on their sense of smell! In fairness they spend a lot of time bumping into things, but they can smell a fly's flatulence from fifty paces." Dotty took another victorious bite from the pie. "I simply followed the smell of horse meat through the castle."

"*Horse* meat?" Arabella grunted. "Blinkin' stinkin' orphans! They told me that pie was pork!"

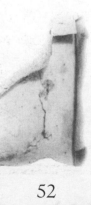

DOTTY DAUNTLESS VS THE CREATURE
(The pitfalls of pretending to be a monster)

It should come as no surprise
That we hide from prying eyes

Signed,
The Creations of Grotteskew

Despite being forced to share her food with Dotty Dauntless, Arabella was clearly impressed by the explorer's talents. She watched with awe as Dotty threw her apple into the air and sliced it into segments with her knife before catching them in her mouth.

Stitch Head, meanwhile, felt altogether more anxious. How did Dotty Dauntless know about the professor? How did she know about the creations? And, crucially, what did she want with them?

"Well, I'm fuller than the time I was guest of gustation at the Sultan of Satsumia's Festival of Fruit!" declared Dotty, leaping to her feet.

"Does — does that mean you're leaving?" asked Stitch Head hopefully.

"Not until I get what I came for!" replied Dotty matter-of-factly. She strode out of Arabella's room into the corridor. "Now, tell me, where are all your monsters? I couldn't help but notice I didn't spot any on my way down here."

"M-monsters? What monsters?" cried Stitch Head. "There are no monsters!"

"Are they caged in your dungeon, perhaps?" mused Dotty, emerging into the castle's cavernous main hall. "Or trapped in your moat, clawing at the walls, desperate to savage all those they encounter? Or lurking in the shadows, ready to leap out and maul us to meatballs with feral ferocity? To bite off our noses and beat us to death with our own legs?"

"No monsters!" cried Stitch Head, glancing around the hall. "No ... monsters ... *anywhere*."

Dotty was right – there wasn't a creation in sight. The castle seemed deserted. Stitch Head breathed a sigh of relief. If Dotty Dauntless was here for monsters, it was better she didn't see any. But where were they?

"You've probably gone and scared 'em off ... all that crashing and banging," explained Arabella, jabbing her finger at Dotty as Pox the monkey-bat landed on her shoulder. "Most of 'em are scared of their own shadow."

"Even though there aren't any!" added Stitch Head quickly.

"Did you say '*scared*', moppet?" Dotty Dauntless eyeballed Arabella. "Unthinkable! Monsters are fearsome and rampant and dreadful and terrible and wild!"

"Not these ones, they ain't. Pox is our most monstrous monster by a million," Arabella tutted, pointing to her monkey-bat. "And he's just misunderstood, ain'tcha, boy?"

"YaBBit!" added Pox.

"You call this delightful little thing a monster?" Dotty retorted, patting Pox on the head as he snapped at her. "No, no, I will need something much more impressive for my purposes. Huge, hulking, savage, but most of all *monstrous!*"

"But they're not like that," said Stitch Head. "I mean, even if there were monsters here, they'd — they'd be gentle and kind, not monstrous at all."

"Not monstrous? Absurd!" scoffed Dotty. "What kind of mad professor would create monsters that weren't even monstrous?"

Arabella shot Stitch Head a look. He instinctively placed a hand on his bag of potions.

"Well, uh, they're not — that is to say — the thing is…" Stitch Head mumbled. He was quite sure the last thing he should do was admit how monstrous the creations were before he cured them. "The *point* is, there's nothing even slightly monstrous about—"

"GROOOAARR!"

The Creature leaped out from behind a pillar, roaring madly and flailing all three of its arms.

"RRAARR! ROARR! GRRAAH!"

"Oh *no*," said Stitch Head. "Creature, this isn't really a good time for—"

"Great thunder! At last!" cried Dotty. "Stand back! I'll handle this!"

"No, wait!" cried Stitch Head, but it was too late – in a flash Dotty Dauntless had drawn her pistol. Before anyone could move, she pulled the trigger.

THUP! THUP!

Two feather-tipped darts shot out of her pistol and landed in the Creature's neck. The Creature stopped dead, its single eye tracking slowly down to the darts.

"GUHH?" it groaned, stumbling back into the middle of the hall.

"The beast still stands!" boomed an incredulous Dotty Dauntless. "Why, that dose would take down a relentlessly raging rhinoceros!"

THUP! THUP!

Two more darts landed in the Creature's chest. It let out a longer, "GUUUHH…" Its eye rolled back in its head, and it toppled backwards on to the ground with a *KRUDD*.

THE VENTURE CLUB

(Dotty's wager)

Here, in the forests of F'shore, I had thought I saw a monster! But in truth it was a lesser-necked burrow badger, resting momentarily beneath a pile of leaves. And so my quest continues. I shall win my wager yet! Great thunder, how can I lose?

Duly extracted from *Dotty Dauntless's Curious Chronicles of Adventuresome Exploration*

"Great thunder, I knew monsters were real!" declared Dotty Dauntless, as the Creature lay unconscious in the middle of the hall. "And this savage beast is perfect for my needs!"

"Creature!" cried Stitch Head. He spun round to face Dotty. "What did you do?"

"'Tis only dazed – I have no use for a dead monster! But my tranquilizer darts will wear off in a few hours," said Dotty Dauntless. She quickly took the rope from around her shoulder and began binding the Creature's claws and feet, looping and knotting with breathtaking speed. "This rope is as strong as my smile is winning – it should hold the monster until my entourage arrives!"

"*Entourage?*" said Stitch Head, panic heaping upon panic. "M-more humans are coming?"

"Oh, not just humans," said Dotty with a wink. She tied the last of a dozen knots and stood back, inspecting the Creature from every angle. "I knew it! I knew I was right! All these years of searching, I knew in my *bones* that monsters were real. And what a glorious specimen of unadulterated beastliness it is!"

"But the Creature isn't like this – I mean, like that!" said a desperate Stitch Head. "It was just pretending!"

"GRuKK!" Pox grunted.

"I think I know unbridled savagery when I see it," scoffed Dotty. "And this wondrous brute has it in spades – I must deliver it to the Venture Club post haste!"

"V-Venture Club?" repeated Stitch Head.

"The greatest collective of explorers the world has ever known!" boomed Dotty Dauntless. "The Venture Club comprises an esteemed group of *ye olde school* adventurers like myself. Between us, we have explored every corner of every continent!"

"What's that got to do with the Creature?" began Arabella, her oversized hat slumping over her eyes.

"Everything and then some, my mad moppet," Dotty replied. "I have two obsessions – monsters and wagers. Great thunder, I have never been able to turn down a bet, especially if the odds are stacked against me, and the boys at the Venture Club know it. Their wager was thus – if I could find a monster before my sixtieth birthday I would be named *The Most Adventurous Explorer in the History of Adventuresome Exploration!*"

"Th-this is all for a *bet*?" said Stitch Head.

"You bet it is!" replied Dotty with a grin.

"My sixtieth birthday is two days away — the Venture Club must be certain of their victory. I cannot wait to see their faces when I return with this behemoth and win my wager!"

"But you — you can't take the Creature!" cried Stitch Head. "You can't!"

"Anyone would think you *wanted* this brutal beast wandering the halls. You should be grateful I'm ridding the castle of— Great thunder, is that the time?" Dotty said, taking a fob watch from her pocket. "I haven't slept in three days — it is only the meditation techniques of the Cult of Kaffeen that have kept me awake this long, and tomorrow is going to be a big day."

With that, Dotty made a beeline back down the corridor to Arabella's room. Before they knew it she'd kicked off her boots and leaped on to the bed.

"Oi!" snapped Arabella. "Get your own bed, you blinkin'—"

"Don't worry, I'll stay on my side — and if it seems as though the sky is falling in the night, it is merely my snoring," said Dotty. "Dawn will be upon us in a scant few hours. Then I shall remove my monster to the Venture Club, and my reputation will be assured!"

With that, Dotty Dauntless lay down and immediately started snoring like a cart rolling over rough cobbles.

"Arabella, she's going to take the Creature!" whispered Stitch Head. He grabbed her arm and dragged her back into the hall where the Creature lay, unmoving. "We have to do something! We have to get it out of—!"

"Boo!" came a cry. A moment later, Ivo popped his head out of the back pocket of the Creature's trousers. "I am winning again!

I am best at game! I am…"

Ivo scratched his head, looking down at the captured Creature. "I am confused," he said. "Are we playing a different game now?"

HIDING THE CREATURE

(Downstairs and up again)

MAD MUSING No. 295

"Why add an arm, when you can add three? And some tentacles and a tail."

From *The Occasionally Scientific Writings of Professor Erasmus Erasmus*

As Dotty Dauntless slept, her snores echoing through the castle, Stitch Head, Arabella and Ivo set about trying to find somewhere to conceal the sleeping Creature. They dragged its hulking bulk through the castle, with Pox flittering above them.

"I do beg your pardon, but is it safe to come out?" whispered a voice from the darkness.

They turned to see half a dozen creations slink out of the shadows. Clover, a mass of colourful wings, long legs and a brush-like tail, was the first to flap into view. "We heard the most terrible racket and all decided to make ourselves scarce," she said. "I didn't even have time to finish my dusting…"

"So, what is it this time?" asked Marjory, a six-armed brain-spider. "Another angry mob? A vengeful spirit? More orphans, perhaps?"

"Nah, it's some old lady," said Arabella, "who's *really* good at smelling stuff."

"Then ... are we safe to come out of hiding?" said Philius, a fish with clockwork feet.

"No!" said Stitch Head with uncharacteristic firmness. "Dotty Dauntless is looking for a monster! If she finds out we have a whole castle full of them, we'll never get rid of her! P-please stay out of sight until we can convince her to leave. *Please* stay in the shadows. And tell everyone ... Dotty Dauntless is *dangerous*."

Stitch Head was right to be cautious about visitors to the castle—especially humans. Apart from Arabella, it had never turned out well. A year earlier, a twisted circus ringmaster named

Fulbert Freakfinder had come knocking on the Great Door of Castle Grotteskew. He was the first human being Stitch Head had ever met (other than the professor, who barely qualified) and had promised Stitch Head fame and fortune beyond the castle, as the star of his *Carnival of Unnatural Wonders*. Stitch Head had let his dreams of a new almost-life blind him to Freakfinder's true scheme – to force the professor to create made-to-order monsters for his freak show. And though Stitch Head had managed to foil Freakfinder's schemes, he had never forgiven himself for putting the professor and his creations in jeopardy.

"Oi! Stitch Head!" yelled Arabella, snapping Stitch Head out of his dreadful daydreams. "Couldn't you have at least got the creations to help us move the Creature before you sent 'em packing? I'm breaking my back here!"

Stitch Head looked around. The castle's creations had already returned to the shadows, leaving him, Arabella and Ivo to continue heaving the Creature to a hiding place. But even with their combined strength, it took them hours to drag their friend to the nearest staircase. Before they knew it, dawn light was starting to seep through cracks in the walls.

"Pulling with only one arm is two times as hard..." puffed Ivo, collapsing to the ground as they balanced the Creature precariously at the top of the stairs.

"We – we can't stop now," wheezed Stitch Head. "Time's running out – we have to hide the Creature before Dotty Dauntless wakes up!"

"*Right*, get out the way, I'll speed things up," panted Arabella, clambering over the top of the Creature and sliding down its rump.

"Speed things— No, wait!" said Stitch Head, grabbing Ivo and scrambling out of the way as Arabella swung her foot hard at the Creature's backside. It teetered on the edge of the steps for a moment — and then toppled down the spiralling stairs.

FLOMP! DOMP! BOMP!

FOMP!

DOMP! FUMP! DOMP!

FUMMPITY!

FOMPITY!

DUMPITY!

DOMPITY—

KRUMP.

"Arabella!" shrieked Stitch Head. "Why did you do—?"

"You just said time was running out!" she growled. "Anyway, I've seen the Creature hit itself over the head with a dining table – it'll be fine."

Stitch Head tore down the stairs as fast as his mismatched legs could carry him.

"Creature! Creature, are you all right?" Stitch Head called, racing to the Creature's side, with Arabella, Ivo and the yapping Pox hot on his heels. "Crea—"

"MORNING!" came a cry. "At least I THINK it's morning, because I just WOKE up, which is STRANGE, because I don't even SLEEP…"

The Creature was sprawled at the bottom of the stairs, still tethered, with a wide grin on its face.

"I JUST had the most WONDERFUL dream," it continued. The Creature clambered to its feet, effortlessly (though unwittingly) snapping Dotty Dauntless's "unbreakable" rope. "I was OUT in the big, WILD world and YOU were there, Stitch Head, and YOU and YOU and I kept saying I want to go HOME, and now I AM and you're all HERE and I'm not going to leave this place ever, EVER ag— Hey, WHY am I at the BOTTOM of the STAIRS?"

"You were shot!" replied Stitch Head. "There's this explorer called Dotty Dauntless and she thought you were monstrous and she tranquilized you and—"

"An EXPLORDER?" the Creature interrupted.

"Uh, yes!" said Stitch Head.

"She TRANQUINIZED me?"

"Well, yes, she—" said Stitch Head.

"Because she thought *I* was MONSTROUS?" said the Creature.

"Yes!" cried Stitch Head.

The Creature scratched its chin with its third arm, and looked thoughtful (or thoughtfully confused). Finally, it beamed and cried, "I KNEW it! I'm the BEST at Let's Pretend We're Monsters!" it boomed.

With that, it bounded back up the stairs, roaring and growling with gleeful madness.

"*Now* where's it going?" huffed Arabella, taking off her hat and wiping her brow.

"Creature, wait!" Stitch Head cried. They all sped after it, but the Creature's great bounding steps took it to the top of the stairs in moments. Then, as they emerged from the stairwell, they heard a familiar...

THUP! THUP! THUP! THUP!

...And watched the Creature slump to the floor once again.

"No..." Stitch Head whispered. "No, no, no..."

"Great thunder, the brute broke my rope and tried to eviscerate me!" Dotty said with a yawn, looming over the unconscious Creature, pistol in hand. "And before I've even had my first cup of tea. What a marvel of monstrousness! What a perfect example of—"

BOOM! BOOM! BOOM!

"What is this terrible noise?" said Ivo. "It cannot be Creature's tap dancing because Creature is unconscious."

Stitch Head recognized the sound immediately. Something was hammering against the Great Door – wall-shaking thuds he could feel in his teeth.

Grotteskew was under attack!

"Oh good, they're here," Dotty cried. "And about time, too!"

THE ELEPHANT

(A cage for a monster)

MAD MUSING No. 9

"No visitors!"

From *The Occasionally Scientific Writings of Professor Erasmus Erasmus*

BOOM! B-BOOM!

"Let's get that door open while it's still in one piece, shall we?" grinned Dotty Dauntless, following the din through the castle.

"*Open* the Great Door? We — we can't!" Stitch Head cried. He hurried after her, instinctively reaching for the key he wore concealed around his neck. "No visitors! No visitors! No visitors!"

"Fret not, little Scamp, they won't be staying long!" said Dotty, striding through the courtyard as Arabella, Ivo and Pox caught up with them.

"Ain't no one opening nothing, Stitch Head," Arabella said. "That door's locked tight and we're the only ones with keys. Yours is around your neck and mine's safe where I left it in ... um... Now, where *did* I leave it?"

"Under your pillow!" Dotty bellowed, brandishing Arabella's key as she reached the castle door.

"Blimey," said Arabella, pushing her hat up on her head. "She's good."

Dotty pushed Arabella's key into the lock and turned it with a *CRUNCH* and a *CLANK*.

"Don't—!" cried Stitch Head, racing for the door as Dotty swung it open.

In an instant, a huge monstrous tentacle reached through the doorway and wrapped itself around Stitch Head's chest. He was immediately hoisted into the air and shaken from side to side, his borrowed bones rattling almost as much as the potion bottles in his bag.

"Stitch Head!" screamed Arabella and Ivo.

"SWaRTiKi!" added Pox.

"Timbo!" said Dotty Dauntless. "Better late than never!"

As he dangled upside down, Stitch Head caught sight of his assailant. His mismatched eyes had witnessed numerous horrors and more than a few wonders … but he'd never encountered anything like this.

A vast, grey-skinned elephant occupied the entire doorway. It was larger than any of the creations, with legs as thick as pillars. Its hide looked as rough and hard as dried earth, and its two majestic tusks protruded menacingly into the courtyard. It grunted loudly, fanning bellow-like ears. Stitch Head had seen a picture of such an animal in one of the professor's childhood story books, but it did no justice to the giant who now held him in its trunk.

"Put him down, Timbo! He's a pet, not a toy!" Dotty instructed.

The elephant grunted angrily before releasing Stitch Head from his grip.

Stitch Head landed with a *PLUD* and an "Uff!"

"Don't mind Timbo – like the milk of the camelopard, he does not travel well," explained Dotty Dauntless, patting the elephant's trunk. "He cannot bear this inclement weather, or the fact that he's thousands of miles from home. But since I rescued him from a pit of quicksand with naught but a piece of string, two coconuts and my own teeth, he has refused to leave my side. He goes where I go, like a loyal pup or a persistent case of dropsy!"

"You've got your own *elephant*?" said an impressed Arabella, as Pox flew around the beast's head with a "GruKK!" and "YaBBiT!"

Stitch Head scrambled to his feet, hoping this was all just a bad dream. But as the elephant squeezed through the Great Door and into the courtyard, things could not have felt more real. Timbo took a few *boom*-ing steps forwards and Stitch Head saw that he was pulling an impressive wagon, the contents of which were concealed under a brightly patterned tarpaulin of every imaginable colour and shade.

"Darkenfire!" cried Dotty Dauntless. "Come and meet my new companions!"

Stitch Head looked up and saw a stout-bodied, spindly legged old man sitting atop Timbo's shoulders. He was wearing a tatty, crumpled version of Dotty's explorer outfit and had an implausibly bushy white beard that seemed to occupy his entire face. The plump passenger clambered awkwardly down from the elephant (Timbo offering his leg as a step) and landed in front of Stitch Head. He surveyed the odd assortment of characters, seemingly without surprise or judgment. Then he bowed slightly and touched the tip of his hat with his fingers.

"Gentlefolk and hoddities, hit is my most profound pleasure to meet you hall," he said, in an accent as thick and impenetrable as his beard. "F. Darkenfire, fellow hexplorer and hassistant to Miss Dotty Dauntless, hat your service."

"H-hello," said Stitch Head, feeling helpless to stop this strange invasion.

"Mr Darkenfire is the reason I am here!" Dotty Dauntless explained, giving Darkenfire an unnecessarily firm slap on the back. "With my sixtieth year fast approaching, I had come to the grim realization that I might *never* win my bet with the Venture Club. Then along came Darkenfire, with tales of Castle Grotteskew and its myriad monsters! He is surely the key to my victory!"

"Hoh no, indeed!" Darkenfire said, his beard jumping up and down as he spoke. "Miss Dotty, you're too kind – I ham but an 'umble servant, keen to follow in the footsteps of hadventuresome hexplorers such has yourself."

Stitch Head nudged Arabella, but dared not ask his question out loud: *how does Darkenfire know about the castle?* He must have glowered at Darkenfire however, because the old man immediately offered an explanation.

"To hilluminate," Darkenfire began. "I recently received a correspondence from a cousin of mine, a hoccupier of this 'ere nearby town of Chuggers Nubbin. He told me the 'ole town was in the grip of *'orrors* … spoke of a castle filled with monsters! I promised myself to steer clear of such a hunspeakable place, but then I hencountered Miss Dotty…"

"And I knew this castle was the answer I had been looking for!" cried Dotty Dauntless. "A way to win my bet!"

Stitch Head felt weak at the knees. Was it possible? Could word of the castle have spread beyond the town? Grubbers Nubbin had endured more than its fair share of monster attacks in recent months – it would be hardly surprising if the townsfolk had been talking about their experiences. What did it mean? Would others be coming to Grotteskew, to exploit his master or try to take over the castle? The thought made his borrowed blood run cold. It felt as if the world was closing in on him.

"Now I'm back in the game and on the verge of glory!" Dotty Dauntless added, grabbing the wagon's tarpaulin. "All I need is a monster to fill *this*!"

With a grand flourish, she tugged the sheet from the wagon. It fell to the ground, revealing a huge iron cage, almost as tall as the elephant itself.

"Oh *no*," whispered Stitch Head.

"Imagine mighty Timbo conveying my discovery through the streets, tongues wagging and minds racing … and the grand unveiling of my monster before the gathered explorers of the Venture Club," cried Dotty Dauntless, banging the bars of the cage. "I'll wager there won't be an un-dropped jaw anywhere!"

Stitch Head pictured the Creature, locked in the cage … dragged through the streets … paraded as some sort of prize.

One way or another, he had to stop them.

THE NINTH CHAPTER

DEEDS

(The inconvenient consequences of preferring mad science to accountancy)

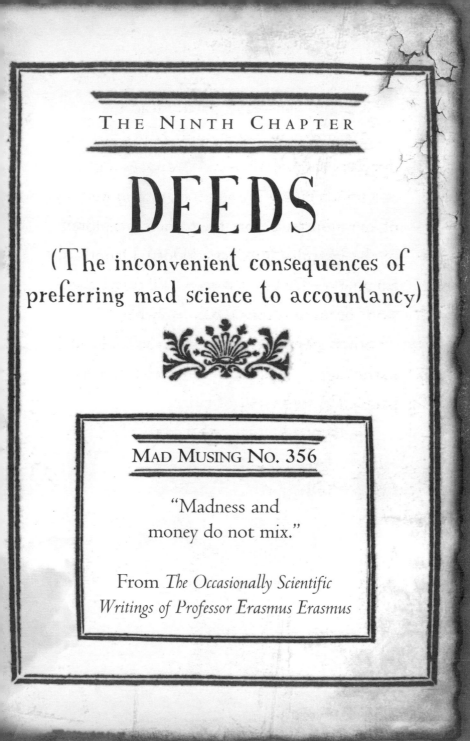

MAD MUSING NO. 356

"Madness and
money do not mix."

From *The Occasionally Scientific
Writings of Professor Erasmus Erasmus*

"Great thunder, let's get my monster into the cage before it awakens! The Venture Club is waiting!" cried Dotty Dauntless, rolling up her sleeves.

"Miss Dotty, perhaps you might permit me a moment's respite," groaned Darkenfire. "I 'ave been steering a particularly pig-headed pachyderm for seven hours straight…"

"Very well, but rest quickly!" ordered Dotty. "I shall load the beast into the cage myself, then we shall away!"

As Darkenfire limped down the corridor (presumably looking for a place to lie down) Stitch Head leaped in front of the cage.

"Please, you can't take the Creature! You just can't!" he begged.

"I am agreeing with this," said the tiny Ivo, joining his side. "You should not do this thing you are planning to do."

"Yeah, what they said!" said Arabella, standing shoulder to shoulder with Stitch Head. "You want the Creature, you're going to have to go through us."

"GRuKK!" added Pox.

As Timbo grunted and readied his trunk to bat them out of the way, Dotty Dauntless just laughed.

"There is no need for grandstanding, friends! I am not a *thief*, nor do I take what is not mine," Dotty Dauntless replied. She raised her voice. "Darkenfire! The deeds, if you please!"

A moment later her valet returned, no more rested than a moment ago (but a bit more disgruntled). Dotty held out her hand and, with a nod, Darkenfire obediently produced a folded piece of paper from a pocket and gave it to her.

"I did not become the world's greatest explorer without learning to plan ahead," said Dotty Dauntless, unfolding the paper carefully. "These are the deeds to Castle Grotteskew. It seems Professor Erasmus was more concerned with mad science than good accountancy and, to cut a long story short, the lease upon the castle lapsed. Which means that, as a result of legal machinations so dull that they would make your hair fall out, your professor is not the legal owner of the castle."

"The castle isn't … the professor … he isn't…?" muttered Stitch Head, beside himself with disbelief.

"What's more, Grotteskew was up for grabs!" added Dotty Dauntless. "So I did what anyone with piles of cash and a can-do attitude would — *I bought it*. You are looking at the proud owner of Castle Grotteskew and everything in it!"

PLACE YOUR BETS

(Stitch Head's wager)

MAD MUSING NO. 882

"Madness is like a rabid racehorse.
It may not win the race, but it
will eat the other horses."

From *The Occasionally Scientific
Writings of Professor Erasmus Erasmus*

Stitch Head took a fearful step forwards, peering at the deeds Dotty Dauntless held out. How could this happen? How could the castle not belong to the professor? There was so much about the land beyond Grotteskew Stitch Head did not know or understand. It felt as if the outside world was spilling like a tidal wave into the castle.

"It – it can't be…" he muttered.

A Deed Indeed

Know Ye That This Deed Writ Hereof Herewith For the Attention and Retention without Pretension Of All Relevant Parties, Peoples and Persons Doth Transfer with Immediately Effective Effect

The Ownership of

Castle Grotteskew

to one

Lady Dorothea Drucilla Dolores Day-Drummond-Day Dauntless

"I am not understanding," said Ivo, as Dotty Dauntless folded the deeds and slid them into her jacket. "Dotty Dauntless *owns* us?"

"Ain't nobody owns nobody, piece of paper or not!" growled Arabella. "You can't own a life!"

"*Almost*-life," Stitch Head added in a whisper, the news ringing inside his brain. Wasn't that Dotty's point? Since the creations were made by the professor, they weren't the castle's residents ... they were nothing more than its contents.

"Will I be needed for this 'ullabaloo, Miss Dotty?" asked Darkenfire. "I could *really* do with a lie-down."

"Rest like the wind, my dear Darkenfire!" replied Dotty. "Once I have conveyed my monster into its cage, we must take our leave!"

"Even if you do own the castle," snapped Arabella, as Darkenfire sloped off again, "there ain't no way you're taking our friend!"

"Friend? For the last time, that creature is a savage monster!" said Dotty.

Timbo grunted threateningly.

"For the last time, it ain't!" snarled Arabella. "But even if it was — which'd actually be more fun, to be honest — it'd still be *our* savage monster."

Savage … that's it, thought Stitch Head, a plan forming almost faster than his mind could race. He took a step forwards and looked up at Dotty Dauntless. "I *bet* you!"

Dotty froze for a moment, as if time itself had stood still. She turned slowly to Stitch Head.

"Did … you … say … '*bet*'?" she cried, her eyes lighting up. "As in, a wager? As in, the staking of that which has value upon an uncertain outcome? Great thunder, now we're talking! Darkenfire!"

After a moment Darkenfire hobbled back into the hall. "Yes, Miss Dotty?" he answered in an exhausted groan.

"Did you hear that? A bet!" Dotty howled. "Little Scamp has a bet!"

"Very good, Miss Dotty – now I'm hoff to rest my bones," he sighed. He slunk away once more and Dotty glowered at Stitch Head.

"I – I bet, um, I bet, uh…" Stitch Head began, wringing his hands and wracking his brain. "I bet I can find a monster even more monstrous than the Creature! Ten times more monstrous!"

"I think I have not met this monster," Ivo said. "It is sounding scary."

"I ain't met them, neither," said Arabella, suspiciously. "What's your game?" she whispered to Stitch Head. "Two minutes ago you didn't even want her to know about the other creations!"

"A monster even *more* monstrous than my monster?" boomed Dotty, beside herself with excitement. "I cannot imagine such a beast, but the possibility intrigues me. Very well, what are your terms?"

Stitch Head scratched the back of his head and took a deep breath.

"If — if I find you a more monstrous monster by the time the Creature wakes up, you take *that* monster instead and leave the Creature here," he explained.

"Stitch Head, what are you——?" Arabella began.

"*And* you give me the deeds to the castle!"

added Stitch Head quickly.

Dotty rubbed her chin thoughtfully. "High stakes indeed! You're my kind of gambler, Scamp! But if you fail, I take my monster, keep the deeds..." She glanced around the room. "And I get the mad moppet's boots!"

"My *boots*? Not a chance!" Arabella howled, jumping into the air with such alarm that her hat slumped over her face. "No way! Ain't nobody having my kicking boots! I wouldn't give 'em for—!"

"Deal!" said Stitch Head.

"*What?*" shrieked Arabella.

"Great thunder, then we have a wager!" replied Dotty, clapping her hands together. "Darkenfire!"

Darkenfire returned yet again, grinding his teeth in frustration.

"*Now* wha— I mean, yes, Miss Dotty?" he snarled.

"It seems we are not in such a hurry after all!" Dotty replied. She turned back to Stitch Head. "You have until my monster awakens ... three hours from now!"

"Now hang on a blinkin'—" Arabella began, but Stitch Head looked at her with such desperation that she stopped in her tracks.

"Trust me, I – I've got a plan!" replied Stitch Head quietly. "I think..."

GATHERING THE CREATIONS

(Buying some time)

MAD MUSING NO. 76

"There is no 'almost-mad'.
Be mad, or be not mad."

From *The Occasionally Scientific
Writings of Professor Erasmus Erasmus*

Stitch Head wasted no time putting his plan into action. First he insisted that Dotty Dauntless and F. Darkenfire remain in the castle courtyard while he located a monster savage enough to serve as the Creature's replacement.

"Stay 'ere, hin this yard, for three hours?" protested Darkenfire. "But ... but there's nowhere for a tired hold man to lay 'is 'ead!"

"It's, uh, for your own safety," explained Stitch Head, crossing his fingers behind his back. "Because of, uh, all the really monstrous monsters."

"Did you hear that, Darkenfire? Really monstrous monsters!" cried Dotty excitedly. "A bet is a bet ... and what a bet! We shall not move from this spot."

With that, Stitch Head, Ivo and a still-fuming Arabella set about gathering the creations in a gloomy ballroom at the most distant corner of the castle. And though many were reluctant to emerge from the shadows, Arabella was more than persuasive. Still, it took almost two hours to gather every last one of the castle's three hundred and thirteen creations, from beetle-bodied bug-boys to headless horses to six-armed slugs.

"Time's ticking on, Stitch Head!" growled Arabella, as the last of the creations filed into the ballroom. She took off her hat and ruffled her hair. "If your plan costs me my boots, Stitch Head, I'm going to kick you *barefoot*."

"GRuKK!" agreed Pox angrily, landing on Arabella's head.

"I also do not understand plan," Ivo confessed, surveying the crowd. "Where are we to find monstrous monster? These ones are all very lovely."

"So why not just *make* a monster?" suggested Arabella. "Why not give the creations the prof's potent potions — I'd be surprised if even Dotty would be able to cage a creation with a belly full of Beast Yeast…"

"We can't, it's too dangerous!" insisted Stitch Head. Beast Yeast was the professor's most powerful potion to date — it turned anything, creation or otherwise, into a savage, uncontrollable monster. Stitch Head had only just managed to develop a cure, and hadn't even had a chance to test it yet. "Anyway, we don't need to find a more monstrous monster — we just need Dotty to *think* we have," Stitch Head continued. "If the creations can *pretend* to be monstrous until the Creature wakes up, then we'll have bought all the time we need. Once they drop the charade, Dotty will finally see there are no monstrous monsters. She'll have no reason to cage anyone, and no reason to stay!"

"Wait, that's your plan? To *fake* it?" howled Arabella in disbelief.

"SWaRTiKi!" concurred Pox, snapping at Stitch Head.

"I like this plan! It is like Let's Pretend We're Monsters!" said Ivo excitedly. "I am best at this game. Are you sure you are not wanting me to be most monstrous monster?"

"Uh…" began Stitch Head.

"But what if Dotty ain't fooled?" asked Arabella. "What about my blinkin' boots?"

"The – the Creature fooled her without even meaning to," said Stitch Head. "Maybe the other creations can do the same."

"Ugh, *fine* – have it your way," growled Arabella. "But good luck getting any of this lot to be monstrous. They're softer than socks!"

Stitch Head took a deep breath and nervously stepped forwards to address the creations.

"Um, hello," he began, so quietly that no one could hear him. "Um, I need your help, to help the—"

"I beg your pardon, would you mind awfully speaking up a tad, old chap?" said a steam-powered skull from the back. "Some of us have no ears, you know…"

"Oi! Shut your gobs!" Arabella barked. She pushed her hat back on to her head. "Stitch Head's telling you his rubbish plan!"

"YaBBit!" Pox echoed.

"Uh, thanks," Stitch Head said, as the creations fell silent. He took another step forwards. "Um, some of you might have – uh, heard about our visitor. Well, she's come here to find a really monstrous monster."

"So, have you told her she's in the wrong place?" asked a hideously huge, seven-armed cyborg serpent with a flaming brain. "I defy you to find anything even approaching monstrous in here."

"The – the thing is," continued Stitch Head, "I've spent my almost-life curing you of your – your monstrous ways … soothing your savagery … removing your rage … mending your madness. But now I need you to remember who you were *before* the remedies and the tonics and the cures – to be the ferocious, untamed monstrosities you were made to be … to be wicked and feral and terrifying ... to be fierce and fearsome and ferocious ... I need you ... to *pretend to be monsters*. Who's with me?"

There was a long, awkward silence. Then:

"Me, be *monstrous*?" said a creation constructed entirely from vital organs. "I don't think I have the guts for it."

"I just can't see myself being vicious," noted a flying eyeball. "Now, if you needed a decorative scatter cushion making, it'd be a different matter..."

"I really prefer fishing to ferocity..." said a brain on wheels.

The creations continued to make their excuses. Before long, some even began to disperse.

"B-but I need your help! Please!" Stitch Head begged. "Dotty Dauntless is going to take the Creature!"

A hush fell over the room. Then:

"The *Creature*? Well, why didn't you say so before, dear chap?" came a cry.

"I'd do anything for the Creature!" said another. "You couldn't ask for a finer creation!"

"The Creature sang at our wedding!"

"It gave us marriage counselling!"

"The Creature brought me out of my shell through amateur dramatics!"

"It's the best after-dinner speaker I've ever known!"

"How can we help? Tell us, do!"

"Huh," said Arabella, putting her hat back on as the noise grew louder. "I didn't see *that* coming."

SCARING DOTTY DAUNTLESS

(The human problem)

We creations live to serve
From ghoul to grimmest goblin
There's no problem we can't solve
But for the Human Problem

Signed,
The Creations of Grotteskew

Stitch Head ended up with more volunteers than he knew what to do with. With the clock ticking on his wager, he narrowed the list to the creations he thought could reasonably pretend to be monstrous and then assembled them in the main hall. They were:

Fulbert, a massive six-armed lizard beast who had (before Stitch Head cured him) been responsible for chasing Fulbert Freakfinder out of the castle, following the scheming ringmaster's foiled kidnap attempt on Professor Erasmus. Though Fulbert had borrowed Freakfinder's forename, he had none of his disagreeable qualities.

Leonora, a hulking hairball with great claws for hands. She was as immense as the Creature, but with the added bonus of having more hair than most of the other creations put together. Her hobbies included musical theatre, topiary and memorizing flags.

Updike, an upside-down-faced octo-monster who lived in the castle moat. He was a truly colossal combination of octopus, sea snake and squid. He was an excellent joke-teller, but didn't like to make his punchlines too funny in case they brought about a case of hysterical vapours.

"Well, they do *look* pretty monstrous, at least," admitted Arabella, surveying the creations as Pox snarled at them judgmentally. "But you'd better convince that old bag you *are* monstrous, 'cause I ain't giving up my kicking boots for *anyone*."

"Plan is good!" added Ivo, leaning against the unconscious Creature as it lay slumped on the hall floor. "As long as Dotty Dauntless does not shoot everyone with—"

"Uh, Ivo, why don't you keep a lookout for Dotty?" interrupted Stitch Head quickly.

"I won't let you down, Stitch Head," said Leonora, as Ivo hurried to the courtyard door. "I've acted in several of the Creature's plays. As a performer, I'm in touch with all my emotional facets, including my savage side. I shall scare this Dotty Dauntless out of her skin!"

"I occasionally catch sight of myself in the mirror and marvel at my many unsettling limbs and distractingly menacing proportions," said Fulbert proudly. "I'm a roar away from scaring myself!"

"And *I* have a vague recollection of trying to kill you, Stitch Head," added Updike, slithering up the wall. "Just before you gave me that Serenity Salve... I've felt quite placid ever since, but for the Creature, I'm sure I can channel the old rage and be *bowel-looseningly* scary."

"Thank you ... thank you so much," said Stitch Head, wondering if this plan might not be as terrible as he first thought.

"Just so long as I can get over the *human problem*," added Updike.

"The human problem?" Stitch Head repeated.

"Oh yes," replied Updike. "Since having to share the castle with one hundred orphans, I'm afraid I've acquired an acute *phobia* of human beings."

"Me too," admitted Leonora. "These days I can't even look at a *picture* of a human without screaming in horror and running away."

"I thought I was the only one!" declared Fulbert. "What a relief! I've been suffering in silence all this time…"

"It's affecting half the castle," said Leonora. "You should come along to one of the Creature's *How to Handle Humanphobia* healing meetings. They're marvellous! A problem shared and all that…"

"Wait, you – you're all terrified of humans?" said Stitch Head.

"Oh yes, absolutely petrified," said Updike with a nod of his upside-down face.

"That's bonkers – what about me?" said Arabella.

"You're *human*?" exclaimed Leonora. "But you're so . . . undomesticated. We all assumed you were a creation that Stitch Head couldn't cure."

"Charmin'!" Arabella sneered. "When this is over, remind me to kick you all in the—"

"Stitch Head! Dotty Dauntless is coming!" interrupted Ivo, his ear pressed against the courtyard door. "Three hours is up! I hear her—"

The door swung open, knocking Ivo to the floor.

"Time's up, little Scamp! Let's see these— Great thunder!" boomed Dotty Dauntless, striding into the room with F. Darkenfire close behind. She peered up at the three massive creations and cast her arms wide in glee. "You were right! A bet well won! Look at how monstrous they—"

"Aieeeeeeeeeeeeeeeeeeeeeeeee!"

A BET IS A BET

(Don't welch on a wager)

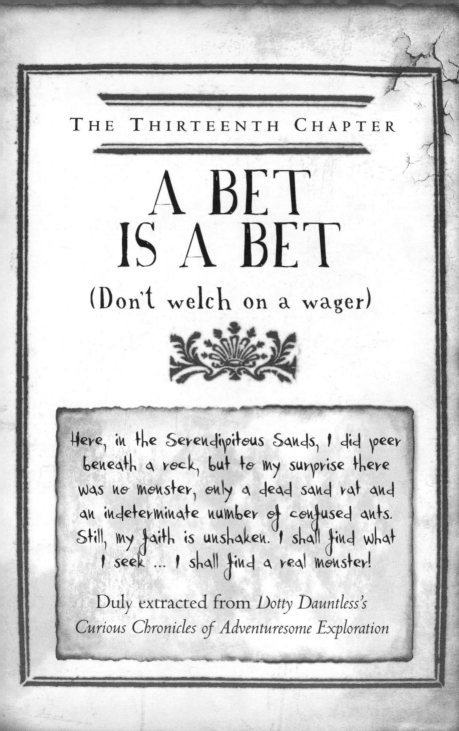

Here, in the Serendipitous Sands, I did peer beneath a rock, but to my surprise there was no monster, only a dead sand rat and an indeterminate number of confused ants. Still, my faith is unshaken. I shall find what I seek ... I shall find a real monster!

Duly extracted from *Dotty Dauntless's Curious Chronicles of Adventuresome Exploration*

At the sight of Dotty Dauntless, the three creations squealed in horror. The sound was even tinier and more mouse-like than the Creature's shrill squeals. Fulbert the lizard-monster immediately turned tail (or tails) and ran out of the room; Updike slithered up on to the ceiling in panic, sweating nervous slime on to the floor and whimpering like a chided dog, while Leonora dived under a nearby table, shaking so hard her hair began to fall out.

"That…" muttered Stitch Head, rubbing his eyes, "didn't go quite as well as I'd hoped."

"You don't say," replied Arabella in a growling whisper. "My potion plan ain't looking so bad now, is it?"

"What a curious paradox," boomed Dotty Dauntless. "They look monstrous enough, but they're as meek as kitten cubs!"

"Hindeed … I can't think what my *cousin* was so scared about," said F. Darkenfire, stroking his beard with obvious concern. "Could it be Mad Professor Erasmus 'as lost his touch?"

"Just — just give me more time!" pleaded Stitch Head. "I'll find you a monstrous monster!"

"I think I'll stick with the one I've got, thanks all the same," Dotty replied, watching Leonora shiver and whimper under the table.

"I suspect the Venture Club will be more inclined to honour our bet if my monster does not squeal like a child who's had its hair pulled. And speaking of wagers…"

She looked at Arabella, and then her gaze dropped slowly to her kicking boots. "A bet is a bet, my little wolverine…"

"Not a chance! These boots is mine! They was given to me by my ol' nan and there ain't nothing in the world that'd make me give 'em up!" protested Arabella.

Pox yapped in angry agreement.

"One must not welch on a wager, moppet!" Dotty declared, closing in. "I have a pair of slippers you can have instead…"

"I ain't wearing no slippers! You'll have to tear these boots off my feet and it'll cost you a face full of teeth!" Arabella snarled, kicking the air wildly. "Aaargh! Raargh! Aar—"

"HEY! Are WE playing Let's PRETEND we're MONSTERS again?" said a familiar voice. "GREAT!"

Everyone spun around.

It was the Creature.

And it was awake!

THE CREATION REVELATION

(Creature comforts ... and discomforts)

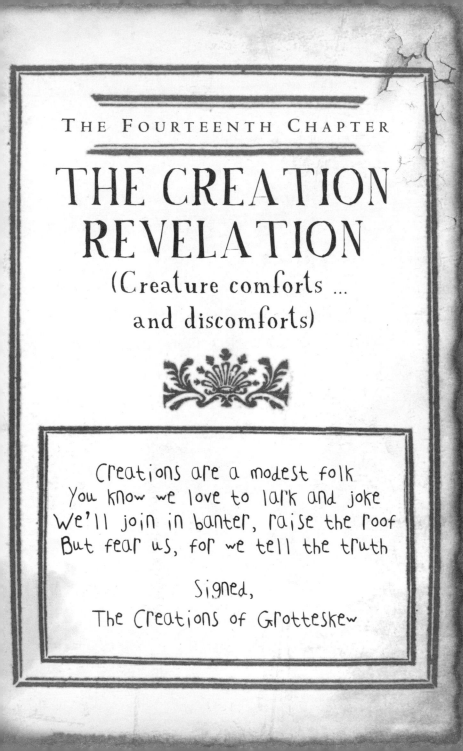

Creations are a modest folk
You know we love to lalk and joke
We'll join in banter, raise the roof
But fear us, for we tell the truth

Signed,
The Creations of Grotteskew

"Creature!"

Stitch Head, Arabella and Ivo all cried the Creature's name as it stretched and yawned.

"Great thunder, my monster's recovered sooner than I thought!" said Dotty Dauntless, drawing her pistol.

"Not again...!" yelped Stitch Head. He grabbed Arabella's hat from her head and flung it at Dotty Dauntless. It knocked the pistol from her hand just as she pulled the trigger:

THUP!

A dart embedded in the wall, inches from the Creature's face. It peered bewilderedly at the dart as Dotty's pistol clattered to the floor.

"Everyone back!" shouted Dotty. "I shall *wrestle* this behemoth if that's what it—"

"I JUST had another WONDERFUL dream!" interrupted the Creature. "I was TRAPPED in a CAGE and I was MILES from home and EVERYONE was STARING at me and— No, wait, that's a TERRIBLE NIGHTMARE! Somebody HOLD ME…"

"My monster, it speaks!" uttered Dotty Dauntless, her mouth agape as the Creature squealed its high-pitched squeal. "And it sounds *ridiculous.*"

"HELLO there!" the Creature boomed, shaking Dotty's hand with its third arm. "I don't believe we've had the TREASURE of meeting! I'm the CREATURE, which isn't really a REAL name, but if I DID have one I think it would be OSCAR or OTIS or ORVILLE or BENJAMIN or BYRON or SHELLEY or SHERMAN and my FAVOURITE things are TICKLING and LAUGHING and STORIES with HAPPY endings and SONGS about FLOWERS and playing Let's PRETEND We're MONSTERS even though I can't play for TOO long because I get NERVOUS…"

Dotty Dauntless took a few steps back, disbelief making her weak at the knees.

"Not monstrous," she muttered in horror. "My monster's not monstrous!"

"I don't mind being the first to say it – we blinkin' told you so," said Arabella, stamping her feet victoriously. "None of 'em are."

"None…?" said Dotty and Darkenfire together, the penny dropping at last.

"Not even one," said Ivo.

Stitch Head quietly breathed a small sigh of relief, and then, for some reason, felt the need to add, "I'm sorry."

"Can I have been deluded?" said Dotty, her heart sinking before their eyes. "Great thunder, perhaps the boys at the Venture Club were right, after all … perhaps this was a fool's errand. Why should one *be* monstrous simply because one *looks* the part? Perhaps the only true monsters are the ones we create, the ones that emerge from the murkier recesses of our own imaginations."

"GRuKK!" barked Pox.

"And now the unthinkable has happened – I have *lost* my wager with the Venture Club," Dotty continued, steadying herself against a wall. "It appears your cousin was mistaken, Fergus…"

"So hit does," replied Darkenfire, staring at Stitch Head suspiciously. "Yet he says he saw them with 'is very own eyes…"

"Sounds to me like your cousin needs glasses!" said Arabella, giving Stitch Head a wink as she replaced her hat on her head.

"OH, you were NEVER going to find any MONSTERS around here," boomed the Creature, putting a sympathetic claw on Dotty's shoulder. "NOT after Stitch Head CURES them all, anyway."

"Cures…?" said Dotty.

"Creature!" whispered Stitch Head.

"Shut it!" added Arabella.

"Stitch Head is TOO modest," added the Creature proudly. "This castle would be TEEMING with MONSTERS if it wasn't for his POTIONS…"

"Great thunder, is this true, little Scamp?" said Dotty, rounding on Stitch Head. "Do you *cure* these monsters of their monstrousness?"

"I-I—" Stitch Head stuttered, grasping his bag of potions tightly.

"Oh, Stitch Head's GREAT at curing creations!" boomed the Creature. "You should SEE how MONSTROUS we all were BEFORE he used his POTIONS on us!"

"And what would 'appen if you *didn't* cure them?" asked Darkenfire.

"Good question! Would they be savage? Feral? Bestial?" Dotty moved toward Stitch Head, her eyes lighting up once more. "Would they be *monstrous*?"

"Well, uh, I suppose, but — but that's not—" Stitch Head muttered, as he found himself backing into a corner.

"We'd be SO monstrous!" replied the Creature. "Just WAIT, the professor's NEWEST creation is going to be AWAKENED any MINUTE now. It's going to be GREAT! And completely TERRIFYING!"

"Creature, *please* stop talking…" whispered Stitch Head, his back now pressed up against the wall.

"Where would I find this new monster? How soon can it be ready? Show me!" said Dotty Dauntless, her face inches from Stitch Head's, a look of mania in her eyes. "Great thunder, we're back in business! I can win my bet after all!"

THE TRUTH ABOUT DOTTY'S WAGER

(High stakes)

I write (to myself, since this is a diary) with news of a wager! The boys at the Venture Club have put to me that I shall not find a real monster by the eve of my sixtieth birthday, but if I do... No, not if! Fie upon "if"! Great thunder, my sixtieth is an age away! I cannot lose! I can almost smell the monstrousness and accompanying glory already!

Duly extracted from *Dotty Dauntless's Curious Chronicles of Adventuresome Exploration*

"Oi! Back off or I'll kick your ears!" interrupted Arabella, pushing her way between Dotty Dauntless and Stitch Head.

"But I need a monster!" cried Dotty in desperation. "I must have a monster!"

"You don't think *I* want to see some proper monsters, roaring and raging and smashing up this place? 'Course I do!" said Arabella. "But if you think you can order Stitch Head around just 'cause you own the castle, you've got another thing coming!"

Arabella clenched her fists and teeth. Dotty Dauntless looked at Stitch Head, fearful and cowed against the wall. She paused, and took a few steps back.

"I'm sorry ... I didn't mean to scare you," Dotty said, her tone suddenly subdued. "But I have spent a lifetime searching for a monster. It has been my dream to find one for longer than I can remember. It has made me reckless." She leaned against the wall as if to steady herself. "I was so sure I would win my wager, that I staked my fortune upon it. Every last penny to my name. Every possession. Everything I own."

"Everything...?" muttered Stitch Head. His skin prickled with fear.

"Everything," repeated Dotty Dauntless. "Including *Castle Grotteskew*."

Stitch Head felt his knees weaken.

"Th-the castle?" he whispered.

"Well, technically I bet the castle *and* everything in it," replied Dotty Dauntless awkwardly. "But only because I didn't think I would lose!"

"B-but this is the creations' home! This is *our* home!" said Stitch Head.

Pox barked in angry agreement.

"Not for long, I'm afraid," replied Dotty. "We explorers are a single-minded lot. Once the Venture Club learn they have won the castle, they will use it to fund their exploring. What they do not plunder themselves, they will sell off — auction to the highest bidder."

"Let 'em try. We'll *fight* 'em for it!" growled Arabella.

"But if the professor doesn't own the castle … then the castle isn't ours to fight for," said Stitch Head, feeling more lost than ever.

"Then what? We just pack our bags and leave?" Arabella growled.

"Per'aps there is hanother way," mused Darkenfire, stroking his beard. He glanced down at Stitch Head. "Per'aps your master is the key to all this."

"The — the professor?" Stitch Head said nervously.

"What are you getting at, Darkenfire?" asked Dotty Dauntless.

"I'm not a hexpert on these matters, Miss Dotty," Darkenfire continued. "But the way I see it, we are in desperate need of a real monster . . . one that 'as *not* been cured. For that we need a beast fresh from the creating table. For *that* we need Mad Professor Erasmus!"

TO CURE OR NOT TO CURE

(A visit to the laboratory)

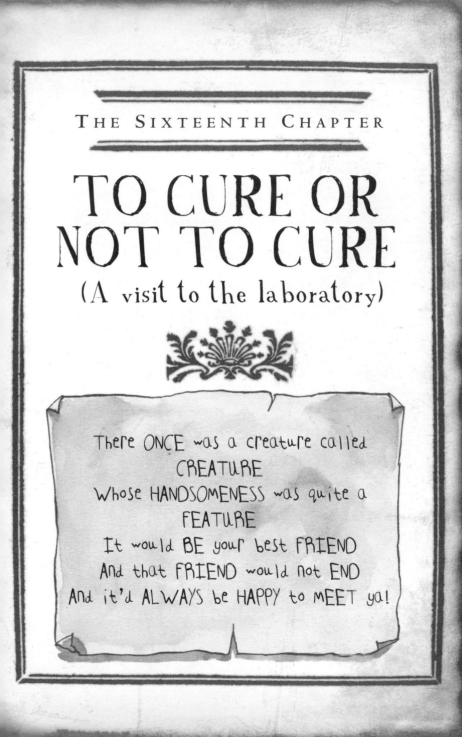

There ONCE was a creature called
CREATURE
Whose HANDSOMENESS was quite a
FEATURE
It would BE your best FRIEND
And that FRIEND would not END
And it'd ALWAYS be HAPPY to MEET ya!

"Aha-ha-ha-HA!"

High above the professor's laboratory, an odd assortment of humans and creations made their way to Stitch Head's favourite place. Sitting in line upon the wooden rafter were Stitch Head, Arabella, the Creature, Ivo, Dotty Dauntless and F. Darkenfire (while Pox flitted about their heads) watching and waiting for the professor to finish his new creation. With their combined weight, the ancient wood of the rafters had started to strain and creak.

"Aha-HAA! Mad science and me, up a tree, E-X-P-E-R-I-M-E-N-T-I-N-G!" cried the professor, cackling as madly as any mad professor had ever cackled. The shape lying on his creating table was undeniably monstrous. It was a horribly huge monstrosity with two equally unpleasant-looking heads, four arms and bony spikes protruding from all over its body.

"Great thunder, how much longer?" said Dotty in a loud whisper, peering through the skylight to the darkening sky. "We've been here for hours! Time is running out ... I need this new monster almost-alive and kicking!"

"He's – he's getting close ... mad science takes time," Stitch Head replied. While he was happy to see his master so immersed in his work, this new creation looked like nothing but trouble. He watched as the professor poured a few drops of a bright red liquid into one of the new creation's feeding tubes. "Beast Yeast," he muttered. "The professor's mixed up another batch!"

Stitch Head patted his potion bag and hoped that his recently mixed bottle of Least Beast potion would counteract its effects.

"Imagine if we all took a swig of that stuff – that poxy Venture Club wouldn't stand a chance against us," said Arabella.

"But I'm a PACIFIST," the Creature said. "I prefer to influence CHANGE through non-violent PROTEST, or an amusing LIMERICK."

"*I* will take terrible beast potion to save castle!" volunteered Ivo. "Perhaps I will grow bigger and bigger and bigger, until I am size of very small child."

"We *can't*," said Stitch Head, so firmly that he immediately blushed a deep grey. "That potion has caused enough trouble already. It's bad enough this new creation is going to be—"

"Monstrous!" interrupted Dotty, excitedly drawing her pistol. "Fear not, my patched-up pal, you don't need to worry about potions and cures. The moment this new horror awakens, I shall tranquilize it to the eyeballs, pop it in the cage and off we go. I win my bet ... and Grotteskew is safe from the Venture Club."

"So if Stitch Head does *not* cure this creation it will mean we are saving other creations?" asked Ivo. "And whole castle?"

"I DON'T see a DOWN side," said the Creature happily. "Although it's HARD to see BOTH sides of ANYTHING when you only have ONE eye."

CREAK...

"The down side is that the creation doesn't deserve to be put in a *cage*," said Stitch Head, as Dotty took aim. "It hasn't done anything!"

"Not yet, it ain't," said Arabella.

Stitch Head turned to her. "Arabella...?" he began.

"Look, Stitch Head," she continued, adjusting her hat. "In no time, that thing down there is going to be a full-blown, rampaging, mad-eyed monster. Maybe this once you could just leave it like the prof meant it to be. Maybe this once you could just let a monster be a monster."

CREEEEAK…

"But…" began Stitch Head … then he sighed. It seemed *everyone* thought Dotty's plan was the best solution. What other choice was there? If Dotty returned to the Venture Club empty-handed, everything would be lost — the castle, the creations, even the professor.

"Live!" cried Professor Erasmus on cue. He approached a bank of machinery covered with levers and switches, which sparked and crackled with energy. "AhahahA! Live!"

Stitch Head instinctively grabbed his bottle of Least Beast from his bag, as Professor Erasmus reached for the levers. He saw Dotty Dauntless take aim…

"Wait," began Stitch Head. "Don't—"

CREEEEEEEEE-AK!

"'Ere," said Arabella, the sound of straining, splintering wood filling the air. "Anybody else hear that?"

A second later, the beam upon which they were sitting gave way ... and the amazed assortment of creations and humans plummeted, screaming, toward the ground.

DROPPING IN ON PROFESSOR ERASMUS

(Stitch Head's master remembers)

I am beginning to lose faith that I shall ever find a real monster. Have I been a fool to think I could find one – to expect it to fall from the heavens and land upon my head?

Duly extracted from *Dotty Dauntless's Curious Chronicles of Adventuresome Exploration*

"MasteaaaAAH!"

Even as he plummeted toward the ground, Stitch Head's first thought was of Professor Erasmus. He landed on top of his master's new creation, before ricocheting off a nearby wall and crashing with a *DUD-UD!* on to the unforgiving stone floor.

"M-master…!" Stitch Head gasped again, struggling to his feet. He looked around and saw everyone splayed on the ground. He quickly accounted for Arabella, Ivo, the Creature, Dotty Dauntless and F. Darkenfire — and even spotted Pox flapping and fretting overhead. But where was Professor Erasmus?

"My HEAD…" groaned the Creature, rubbing its great, hairy crown as it sat up, "…Is totally FINE! Just ONE of the BENEFITS of having a skull that's NINETY-TWO percent solid BONE."

"Mmmff!"

"My BOTTOM is making a strange NOISE though," the Creature added, looking down. "Maybe I SHOOK something LOOSE down there…"

"Mmmff!" said the Creature's bottom again.

"Creature, get up!" cried Stitch Head, racing over as it scrambled to its feet.

Splayed out on the floor where the Creature had landed was Professor Erasmus.

"Master!" Stitch Head shrieked, cradling his master's head in his tiny, mismatched hands. Professor Erasmus lay still.

"Professor Erasmus!" cried Darkenfire, as everyone gathered round. "His 'e all right?"

"He must be! He still has a monster to awaken!" added a desperate Dotty Dauntless.

"CURSE my WELL-developed PHYSIQUE!" boomed the Creature. "If ONLY I hadn't spent SO long TONING up my RUMP, it might have BEEN more SQUISHY…"

Stitch Head held his master for a long, silent moment. Then, at last, a wheezing hiss of air escaped slowly from the professor's mouth and he began to stir.

"Master! Master, are you all right?" Stitch Head cried. "Speak to me, Master!"

"I – I… " Professor Erasmus gasped, his eyes slowly opening. "I … *remember* you."

"Y-you do?" stuttered Stitch Head. He dreamed of these moments! He could count the number of times his master had looked at him with even vague recognition on one hand. A cautious smile crept across his face.

"Yes, Master. It's me," he said. "It's Stitch Head."

"Not … *you!*" the professor wheezed. He struggled to raise an arm and pointed a bony finger, waggling it weakly. "You!"

"Who, ME?" said the Creature.

"Or me?" suggested Dotty Dauntless.

"It ain't me … I don't think," said Arabella.

"Is it I?" said Ivo.

"YaBBit?" said Pox.

"No, no, no…!" the professor groaned, jabbing his finger at the air. "Him!"

Everyone turned.

The professor was pointing at F. Darkenfire.

THE LIFE-LEVER
(To pull or not to pull)

MAD MUSING No. 119

"I mean it! No visitors!"

From *The Occasionally Scientific Writings of Professor Erasmus Erasmus*

"I ... remember ... you..." the professor wheezed one last time, before Stitch Head felt his master's head grow heavy in his hands as he slipped into unconsciousness.

"Master ... you'll be all right," he whispered. Then he turned to face Darkenfire, his eyes narrowing. "What – what did he mean, he remembers you?"

"I – I dare say I 'aven't a clue! I've never met 'im, not hin all my days!" said Darkenfire, nervously patting his beard.

"Is that so?" added Arabella. "How could the prof remember you if you ain't never met?"

"And you knew about the castle," said Stitch Head. "You told Dotty Dauntless about the creations..."

"AND you came here on an ELLY-PANT," added the Creature, trying to join in. "Very SUSPICIOUS."

"The professor's mad! Why, hit's in 'is job description!" protested Darkenfire, edging backwards. "They're changing the subject, Miss Dotty! What about the monster? Your birthday happroaches!"

"Great thunder, you're right! We need this monster alive and kicking!" Dotty boomed. "And roaring and snarling, if we can manage it."

"There's nothing we can do!" replied Stitch Head firmly, still cradling his master's head. "The professor is in no fit state to do anything! Look at him!"

"Then we shall have to bring it to life ourselves!" said Dotty. She paced over to the great bank of levers and inspected them. "Now which one should I pull…?"

"No, don't touch anything!" Stitch Head cried, leaping to his feet. "If you pull the wrong lever it'll create a power surge! You could blow up the whole laboratory!"

"It's worth the risk!" Dotty howled. She lunged for the lever. "I need this monster … *we* need this monster!"

"He said no, you mucky rotten goat!" cried Arabella, as she, the Creature and Ivo leaped in between Dotty and the control panel, blocking her path. Arabella folded her arms.

"This is *Stitch Head's* castle, whatever some piece of paper says! And what he says goes!"

"Even if it means you lose the castle? Even if it means you lose *everything*?" asked Dotty in disbelief.

"That's up to Stitch Head," replied Arabella. "Apart from the prof, he's the only one who knows which lever to pull."

"He does?" said Dotty Dauntless, spinning around to face Stitch Head. "Then what are you waiting for? Pull it, little Scamp! Pull the lever!"

Stitch Head stared at the control panel. Arabella was right — all he had to do was pull the life-lever and the professor's new creation would be awakened. Dotty would have her monster, and the castle would be safe from the Venture Club.

"Ain't no one decides this but you, Stitch Head," said Arabella, stepping aside.

"But whatever you are choosing, it is OK with us," added Ivo.

"We'll STICK by you," added the Creature. "Like when I accidentally GLUED myself to you that time."

"I…" Stitch Head began. It barely felt like a choice at all. How could he *not* bring this creation to almost-life, if doing so meant saving the castle? How could he lose everything for the sake of one creation, which wasn't even almost-alive yet and was likely to try and savage him the minute it was awakened?

He walked slowly over to the control panel as the others stood aside. For the longest time, he peered at the life-lever. Then he reached out a tiny hand toward it.

He paused.

"I – I'm sorry," he said. "I can't."

Stitch Head slumped to the floor.

"I – I know what it's like to be locked away," he said quietly. "If awakening that creation means it spends an almost-life in a *cage*, I can't do it. No one deserves that."

Arabella, the Creature, and Ivo let out a collective sigh, while Dotty Dauntless placed a hand on Stitch Head's shoulder.

"I believe I have failed to appreciate how very *human* you creations are," she said. "But, great thunder, what a pickle. We're more pickled than the Pickle Picking People of Preservia ... and I can't help but feel partially responsible."

Stitch Head looked up at Dotty Dauntless, a tear in his eye.

"All right ... *totally* responsible," Dotty added with a sigh.

"I'm sorry, too," said Stitch Head. He put his head in his hands. "What are we going to do? Where are we going to go? This castle is all my master has ever known. The only time he's ever left is when he was *kidnapped* by ... by... Oh *no*."

A flash of realization suddenly burned in Stitch Head's eyes. He glanced over to where the professor lay ... except he wasn't there. He was gone.

And so was F. Darkenfire.

F. DARKENFIRE'S SECRET

(The man behind the beard)

Today I encountered a portly, aged gentlefellow with a most considerable beard by the unlikely name of F. Darkenfire. I had little time for him at first, but then he spoke a word, a single word, which caught my attention and freshened the breath of my brain. The word was MONSTERS.

Duly extracted from *Dotty Dauntless's Curious Chronicles of Adventuresome Exploration*

"No, no, no! Why didn't I see it before?" cried Stitch Head, his eyes wide in horror. He looked up and saw the door to the laboratory swinging on its hinges. "He's taken him! Master!"

"What is happening or has happened, Stitch Head?" asked Ivo.

"And where is my hirsute helper?" said Dotty, looking around. "Darkenfire? Darkenfire!"

"He took him! He took the professor!" Stitch Head cried in desperation. "We have to find them, now!"

"Great thunder, I'm confused," confessed Dotty Dauntless. "But *finding* is something I can most certainly do. Darkenfire has always carried the most distinct smell of greasepaint." She took a long sniff of air and added, "Got him! Follow me!"

Everyone hurried after Dotty as she followed her remarkable nose through the castle and up the spiralling stairs, all the way to the top of the castle.

"I've been such an idiot!" muttered Stitch Head, trying to keep up. "All this time, it's been staring me in the face!"

"WHAT has?" asked the Creature from behind him. "Your REFLECTION?"

"How else could he know so much about the castle – unless he'd *already been inside*," Stitch Head continued. "And Dotty was his way back in!"

"Whose way back in where?" asked Arabella. "What are you on about, Stitch Head?"

As they raced out on to the ramparts, Stitch Head's dread turned to abject terror. The rumble of engines and the whirr of motors filled the air. Through the encroaching gloom, he saw Dotty Dauntless's flying machine at the other end of the ramparts. And busily loading the unconscious professor into the flying machine's cockpit, was F. Darkenfire.

"What is Darkenfire doing with the professor?" asked Ivo.

"That's not Darkenfire... There *is* no Darkenfire!" cried Stitch Head. "'F. Darkenfire' spells *Freakfinder*!"

"Lugs and mumbles, I'm found out! But you're too late!" howled Darkenfire, spinning around. He grabbed hold of his hat and great white beard and threw them off to reveal a gleaming bald head and long, twirling moustache.

"Great thunder, he's as bald as a baboon's bottom!" cried Dotty.

"That's Fulbert blinkin' Freakfinder! He's been after the professor for ages — wants him to make monsters for his cruddy carnival!" roared Arabella. "Freakfinder, you no-good, scheming bog-head! Give us back the prof or I'll kick your nose off!"

"You ain't getting him, and you ain't getting me!" cried Freakfinder, clambering into the flying machine and strapping himself in.

"Stop!" shouted Stitch Head, racing toward the flying machine as its wings began to beat.

"I told you, you little snot!" laughed Freakfinder. "I told you I'd get the professor in the end!"

"No!" Stitch Head cried, as the flying machine took to the air and cleared the castle. Without stopping to think, he ran toward the edge of the wall ... and jumped off the top of the ramparts.

FIGHT OR FLIGHT, OR BOTH

(Duel in the skies)

Great thunder!
I have built myself a flying machine!
What could possibly go wrong?

Duly extracted from *Dotty Dauntless's*
Curious Chronicles of Adventuresome Exploration

Stitch Head heard Arabella cry his name as he leaped from the castle walls. He reached out a tiny hand for the flying machine's landing wheel.

"Urf!" he cried, grabbing hold. He glanced down and saw the hill, far below him and shrinking as the flying machine soared upwards.

"Lugs and mumbles, this ain't a taxi cab! Get off!" hissed Freakfinder from the cockpit. He swiped at Stitch Head with a stubby arm, but he was out of reach.

"G-give me back the professor!" said Stitch Head, although he had no idea what he would do with him if Freakfinder obliged.

"Fat chance! Do you know how much plannin' and plottin' I've put into this?" snarled Freakfinder. "For *months* I've been down on my luck, trying to fathom a way back into the castle, to get my mitts on your monster-makin' master! I'd all but given up hope – then I heard tell of Dotty Dauntless, an eccentric explorer with more money than sense and monsters on her mind…"

"S-stop…!" Stitch Head pleaded, unable to do anything but cling on for almost-life.

"I wasted no time in trackin' her down … I knew from that moment, Dotty Dauntless was my key back into Castle Grotteskew," Freakfinder continued. "Once I promised her monsters, she couldn't get to the castle quick enough! All I needed was a simple disguise to fool you and your snot friends when I got 'ere…"

Stitch Head looked down and saw they were already soaring over Grubbers Nubbin. With every ounce of his strength, he began pulling himself toward the cockpit.

"Figured I'd just find the professor quick sharp and make my escape with him on this flyin' machine," Freakfinder went on, bellowing his monologue against the loud hum of the engines. "But between that bothersome bag and *your* bloomin' bet I never got a chance ... not 'til we literally fell on the professor's head!"

"I'll ... s-save you ... Professor..." muttered Stitch Head, edging closer to Freakfinder.

"Now your master is going to make me all the freaks I need for my *Carnival of Unnatural Wonders!*" Freakfinder laughed. "And you ain't going to cure them! They're goin' to be real monsters ... and they're goin' to make me rich!"

"No!" Stitch Head cried, grabbing the controls. The flying machine lurched and dived toward the ground.

"Lugs and mumbles! You don't know when to throw in the towel! Off, I said!" growled Freakfinder. He grabbed Stitch Head by the scruff of his neck and flung him on to the nose of the flying machine. Stitch Head skittered along it, just managing to grab hold of the front of the machine before he plummeted to the ground. He held on desperately, his legs dangling in the air.

"I'll grind you into dust and stitches! Death by Chuggers Nubbin!" Freakfinder cried with a grin, aiming the flying machine at the buildings below.

Stitch Head looked down and saw the roofs of houses rushing up to meet him.

"Uh-oh," he whispered. "*No.*"

Stitch Head tucked in his knees and heard a

KROOORNCCCCHH

as the front wheels scraped along one of the roofs, which disintegrated in a mass of wood and slate. Stitch Head scrabbled back up the nose, shattered roof tiles flying past his face. As Freakfinder banked back up into the air, Stitch Head managed to grab hold of one of the wires connecting the cockpit to the balloon.

"Little snot! I'll shake you off!" shrieked Freakfinder. He dragged the controls to the left and the flying machine pitched again, flinging Stitch Head backwards and forwards like a rag doll. He felt his grip on the wire weaken.

"S-s-stop…" he whimpered, as he heard the *clink-clink* of the potions in his bag.

The potions!

He looked up and saw the taut, egg-shaped balloon above him. As he held on tightly with one hand, he reached the other into his bag, pulled out the bottle of Least Beast and held it by the neck. Then he smashed it against the side of the cockpit. It shattered with a *TISSH!* and the potion spilled into the air.

"Oi! What are you doin'?" snapped Freakfinder, his eyes on the skies. Stitch Head did not answer. As he felt his fingers slip, he looked up at what remained of the jagged, broken bottle … and thrust it into the balloon.

The balloon gushed air and seemed to shrivel and shrink in an instant. The flying machine listed in the air before dropping like a stone.

"Mad thing! We're going down!" howled Freakfinder, wrestling with the controls and desperately trying to slow their descent as the machine spun in the air. Stitch Head felt his stomach lurch and wrench.

He saw the professor, still unconscious in the passenger seat, and began to drag himself slowly toward the front of the flying machine. As he reached out for his master, he saw tops of trees and then ground.

"Lugs and—!"

AFTER THE CRASH
(Freakfinder vs everyone)

MAD MUSING NO. 34

"There's nothing like a potion
to cause a commotion."

From *The Occasionally Scientific
Writings of Professor Erasmus Erasmus*

The flying machine drove into the ground, churning up great sods of earth before colliding with a tree. Finally, it skidded to a clumsy halt.

"Master...?" whimpered Stitch Head, his head spinning. He'd been thrown clear of the flying machine. Debris from the crash was strewn across the ground, and what remained of the machine lay crumpled and upturned in a field of tall grass just outside Grubbers Nubbin. As Stitch Head dragged himself to his feet, he saw a figure pull itself out of the wreckage.

"M-master?" he groaned.

"No, it's not, little snot!" came the reply. It was Freakfinder. He eyeballed Stitch Head. "You've been nothing but trouble since I first set my unfortunate eyes on you! Why can't you just leave me to pilfer your professor in peace?"

"Won't … let you…" muttered Stitch Head, limping weakly toward the wreckage of the flying machine. "Master…"

"You patchwork pest, I'm goin' to put an end to your insistent interferin' once and for all," Freakfinder hissed. He retrieved a metal bar from the ground, which moments ago had made up part of the flying machine's frame. He paced toward Stitch Head, slapping the bar repeatedly against his palm. "And don't worry, I'll take good care of your master – at least until he's served his purpose."

"No…!" Stitch Head yelled. He ran at

Freakfinder, but with a swing of the metal bar Freakfinder scooped up Stitch Head's legs and sent him crashing face first into the ground.

"Give my regards to the afterlife," Freakfinder said, raising the bar high over his head. "If that's where *freaks* like you end up…"

"Oi, Freakfinder!"

Freakfinder turned.

There was an elephant charging toward him.

"Aaargh!" Freakfinder screeched as Timbo reared up in front of him, trumpeting wildly. He didn't notice the passengers riding on the elephant's back – Arabella (still wearing her safari hat and looking for all the world like a young Dotty Dauntless), the Creature, Ivo and Dotty herself – all he saw was the elephant's mighty trunk as it swung toward his face. A moment later Freakfinder found himself flying through the air.

"YuRF!" he cried, bouncing with a *PLUD-UD!* off the trunk of a nearby tree.

"Great thunder, Darkenfire — or whomever, in truth, you may be," said Dotty Dauntless, as she and Arabella leaped down from the elephant. "What's the meaning of this nefarious, albeit decidedly adventurous, behaviour?"

"You mad old bag!" Freakfinder wheezed, scrabbling to his feet. "You served your purpose when you got me into the castle. Now back off! You ain't taking me without a fight!"

"There's NO need for FIGHTING," insisted the Creature. "I've written a TOUCHING and HILARIOUS poem that should put ALL of this into PERSPECTIVE…"

"Stinkin' pig-face!" snarled Arabella, rolling up her sleeves. "I'm gonna kick you so hard your socks come off!"

"Back, the lot of you!" Freakfinder snapped. "Back, or else I take a swig of *this*."

He reached into his pocket and took out a small red bottle, brandishing it like a weapon.

Everyone froze.

"Beast Yeast ...

he must have taken it from the laboratory," whispered Stitch Head. "P-please, don't drink it!"

"He ain't got the guts!" shouted Arabella. "I should shove that whole bottle down your neck, save you the trouble of drinking it!"

"Trouble?" sneered Freakfinder. A maniacal grin spread across his face as he popped the cork from the top of the bottle. "Lugs and mumbles, I'll show you trouble."

"Don't—!" yelled Stitch Head again.

But he did. Freakfinder poured the liquid down his throat in one glug.

"AuuuurrUUUuUAUAAAGH!" he cried, falling to his knees. All at once, the crunch of shifting bones and the taut creak of stretching muscles filled the night air. Freakfinder doubled in size and doubled again, hair and bones exploding from his body. In moments, he had changed – suddenly, violently – into a *monster*.

GROOWRR!

Freakfinder reared up, his mad roar filling the air. He was covered in black-and-white striped fur, his eyes glowed red and curled

horns protruded from his head. His huge
mouth was a mass of sharp teeth, framed by
an altogether monstrous moustache.

In that moment even the mighty Timbo was paralyzed with fear. Stitch Head instinctively reached into his potion bag, but he had shattered his bottle of Least Beast to burst the flying machine's balloon. He looked up as Freakfinder loomed over them, baring jagged teeth.

"Everyone, RUN!" cried Stitch Head.

"Where's the adventure in that?" said Dotty Dauntless with a grin.

With that, she drew her pistol and took aim.

THUP!
THUP!
THUP! THUP! THUP! THUP!
THUP! THUP! THUP! THUP!

JUST WHEN YOU THOUGHT YOU COULDN'T FIND A MONSTER
(Return to the castle)

Here, in the Mires of Misleadia, did I venture forth into a cave, for I was sure I glimpsed a most monstrous monster within. But in truth it was naught but a patch of moss. Great thunder! Shall I ever find a real monster? Does such a thing even exist?

Duly extracted from *Dotty Dauntless's Curious Chronicles of Adventuresome Exploration*

By the time Dotty Dauntless had emptied a dozen tranquilizer darts into the Freakfinder-monster, he looked rather like a particularly savage pincushion.

GROOORRRR...?

Freakfinder swayed for a moment, before his red eyes rolled back into his head, and he fell, face first, to the ground.

"Did you see that? It cost me every dart I had to floor him!" cried Dotty Dauntless with glee. "What a beast! What a behemoth! What a *monster!*"

"Nice shooting!" said an impressed Arabella. "But I still think you should've let me kick his socks off."

"VIOLENCE solves NOTHING," explained the Creature. "EXCEPT in this instance."

"Everyone is all right?" asked Ivo. "Where is professor?"

"Professor!" cried Stitch Head, racing over to the upturned flying machine. With a nod from Dotty Dauntless, Timbo strode over to the machine, wrapped its trunk around the cockpit and effortlessly turned it over. The professor's unconscious body flopped out and on to the ground.

"Master!" cried Stitch Head. "Talk to me, Master!"

A long moment passed ... but the professor lay still.

"He is … he is not all right?" whimpered Ivo. Then a dry wheeze escaped from the professor's mouth, and his eyes slowly began to open. Professor Erasmus peered at his first creation.

"You…" he said, staring deep into Stitch Head's wide, teary eyes. "Do I know you?"

Stitch Head breathed a long sigh of relief, and turned back to his friends.

"He's all right," he said with a smile.

+++++++++++++++++++++++++++++

Dotty Dauntless's faithful elephant carried everyone back to the castle, and dragged the sleeping Freakfinder-monster by the tail with its mighty trunk. The sky was dark by the time they made their way through the Great Door into the courtyard … and Professor Erasmus was feeling altogether more himself.

"Bah! All these interruptions are intolerable!" he howled, as Timbo raised a leg to help them climb down. "I must get back to my experiments! I have a creation on the boil! Surely my greatest creation ever! Ah-ha-ha-HAA!"

Stitch Head watched his master hurry back to his laboratory, and then climbed down from Timbo's back.

"I suppose I'd better fetch another couple of bottles of Least Beast from the dungeon," he said. "One for his new creation, and one for Fulbert Freakfinder."

"And THEN we'd better start LOOKING for a new HOME," said the Creature. "I'd like somewhere with a ROCKERY…"

"Now hang on a minute," said Arabella. "Like you said, Stitch Head, caging a creation ain't right. But *Freakfinder* ain't no creation."

"Great thunder, you angel of unkemptness! You're correct!" declared Dotty, pointing at the sleeping Freakfinder. "This is exactly the sort of savage, uncontrollable monster I need to win my bet! And what poetic justice for the deceitful fiend!"

"But … we can't just *leave* him like this! We can't just leave him as a *monster*," said Stitch Head. "Can we?"

Arabella folded her arms and raised an eyebrow. "If it means saving the castle, the creations and that mad old lizard you call a master," she replied with a grin. "You bet your ice-blue eye we can."

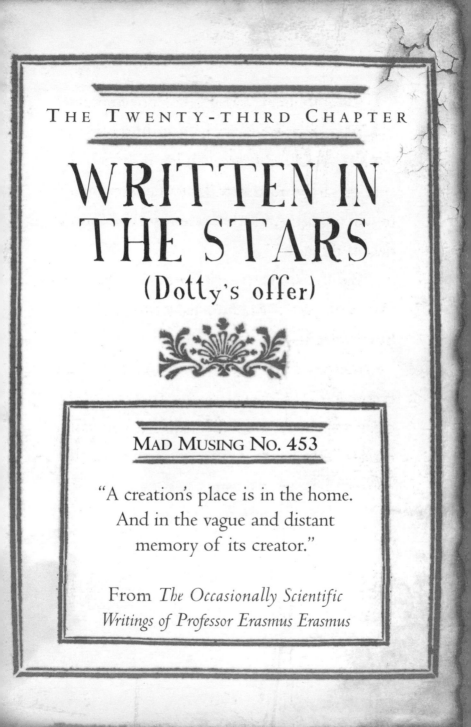

WRITTEN IN THE STARS
(Dotty's offer)

MAD MUSING No. 453

"A creation's place is in the home.
And in the vague and distant
memory of its creator."

From *The Occasionally Scientific
Writings of Professor Erasmus Erasmus*

The stars filled the night sky once more. Arabella had been watching Dotty Dauntless and Timbo load and secure the Freakfinder-monster into his cage for half an hour, ready for transportation to the Venture Club.

"Great thunder, the boys at the club will spit out their port when they set eyes upon my monster!" Dotty boomed, admiring it. "Though I do wonder where I shall keep him..."

"Uh, about that..." said Stitch Head, limping into the courtyard with the Creature and Ivo behind. All three had new cuts and bruises from administering a healthy dose of Least Beast to the professor's latest creation.

"Blimey, you lot look worse for wear," said Arabella, stroking a purring Pox. "How's the new monster?"

"He's GREAT! Now he's NOT trying to EAT us," said the Creature. "His name is ARCHIBALD. He likes WATERCOLOUR paintings and CROSSWORD puzzles."

"*And* we didn't even use all of this," Stitch Head said, taking a small red bottle out of his bag and handing it to Dotty. Upon it were the words:

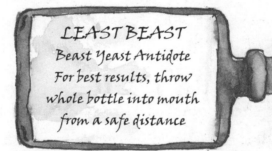

LEAST BEAST
Beast Yeast Antidote
For best results, throw
whole bottle into mouth
from a safe distance

"A cure? After all the trouble he caused you?" Dotty said, inspecting the bottle.

"I know, but..." Stitch Head began. "No one deserves to spend their life in a cage."

"What a good pup you are, little Sca— Stitch Head," said Dotty, dropping the bottle into her pocket. "I'm sorry I brought you quite so much trouble."

"So, when are you leaving?" asked Arabella, giving the wheels of Dotty's wagon a gentle kick. "Back to the big, wide world…"

"As soon as I finish adding a few more locks, and polish the bars up just so," Dotty replied. She peered at Arabella for a moment. "You know, I find myself without an assistant, and I could use someone with your spirit, moppet. Tell me, have you ever gazed at the stars and dreamed of excitement?"

"What, stargazing? I'm an *expert*," replied Arabella proudly. She pointed at the constellations. "See there? That's the *Damp Sock*, over there's the *Dry Bogie*, and that there's the *Washing-Up Bowl*…"

"Great thunder, what an imagination!" laughed Dotty Dauntless. "But look there!

Can't you see the *Massive Monster of Moaroar?* The *Beast of Bignosia?* The *Big-Booted, Four-Footed Behemoth?* So many monsters yet to discover!"

"You see monsters?" said Arabella, peering into the sky. "I'd almost forgot they was up there..."

"Why, the stars are filled with monsters — among other things!" replied Dotty. "There's also the *Jungle of Ancient Secrets* ... the *Temple of Hidden Futures* ... the *Cave of Undiscovered Knowledge*. Life is a wide and wonderful adventure, Arabella, and it's waiting for whomsoever is brave enough to step out into the unknown ... and hopefully find a *monster* or two in the bargain. Great thunder, the world is a *gift*, and if you are lucky enough to live in it, then you must grab it with both hands!"

"This is easy for you to say," said Ivo, staring at his single arm.

"It DOESN'T sound as much FUN as Let's Pretend We're Monsters ANYWAY," added the Creature loudly.

"So, what do you say, Arabella?" Dotty added. "All I can guarantee is awe-inspiring exploration and non-stop adventuring! Would you care to join me?"

Arabella suddenly fell quiet. Stitch Head hadn't seen her like that since the time she had her spirit stolen by a soul-sucking spider-monster. It was more than a little unnerving. Then, finally, she took off her safari hat and handed it back to Dotty Dauntless.

"Nah," she said. "That life ain't for me."

Stitch Head wasn't at all sure that she meant it. He felt like something had changed.

"I respect your decision!" Dotty cried, placing the hat on her own head. Then she handed Arabella back her key. "Perhaps one day we shall meet again!"

"Yeah…" replied Arabella, just loud enough for Stitch Head to hear. "Maybe."

DOTTY'S DEPARTURE

(The big, wide world)

Are monsters real, I wonder?
Great thunder, how I wonder!

Duly extracted from *Dotty Dauntless's*
Curious Chronicles of Adventuresome Exploration

It was Arabella who opened the Great Door
for Dotty Dauntless. She looked distant and
strange as she watched the explorer guide her
elephant-drawn wagon through the doorway.

"Farewell, one and all!" Dotty boomed.
She climbed on to Timbo's back and they
began tramping down the hill. "Look after
my castle for me!"

Stitch Head sidled over to Arabella, as she looked up at the stars.

"I-I never really noticed the stars before I met you," he said. "Now I don't think I'll ever look at them in the same way again. Maybe — maybe once you've seen something differently, you can't see what you used to see."

"I s'pose," she said, peering at Stitch Head. "'Ere, what are you blatherin' on about, anyway?"

Stitch Head wasn't sure if he could say what he was about to say, but then he heard the words leave his mouth.

"Do — do you want to go with Dotty Dauntless?"

Arabella turned to Stitch Head. She ruffled her hair and stared at him, a lost look in her eyes.

"I hadn't even thought about it until she

asked me," she said at last. "Now I can't think of nothing else."

"Oh…" Stitch Head said quietly. He took a deep breath. "Because I belong here, Arabella — I was *made* to be here … but you weren't made. You were *born* into the big, wide world. And like Dotty says, it's yours for the taking."

"I ain't hardly been nowhere but Grubbers Nubbin," she said. "Then after my ol' nan went and died, you gave me somewhere to call home again. I ain't never going to forget that."

"I know. And wherever you go, you'll always have a home here," said Stitch Head, wiping a tear from his eye. "And – and you'll always be my best friend."

Arabella sniffed. Then she handed Pox to him. The monkey-bat immediately started to growl and snap at Stitch Head's fingers. Dotty's wagon was already making its way down the hill.

Arabella leaped to her feet.

"Oi, Dotty, wait!" she cried – and raced after her.

MORE AT HOME THAN EVER

(Kicking without boots)

The Adventure is my greatest friend,
for it is full of surprises.

Duly extracted from *Dotty Dauntless's*
Curious Chronicles of Adventuresome Exploration

Stitch Head made his way to the Great Door as it creaked on its hinges, and watched Arabella run full-pelt after Dotty's wagon. Before long he lost sight of her in the darkness. Tears welled in his eyes. He waited a few moments more. Then he pushed the door closed, took out his key and locked it.

"Has DOTTY gone ALREADY?" said the Creature. "I was going to ASK if she wanted to PLAY our new GAME, Let's Pretend We're EXPLORDERS!"

"I am best at this game," said Ivo from the Creature's jacket. "I have explored all Creature's pockets already. I found twig *and* ball of lint!"

"She's ... she's gone," replied Stitch Head.

"YaBBit!" barked Pox, snapping at the Creature's ankles.

"OH well," said the Creature. "MAYBE

Dotty will be BACK one day. No ONE can stay AWAY from here for LONG. Look at FERBERT FREAKENFIRE – he LOVES it here…"

"I – I don't mean Dotty," said Stitch Head. "She – she's gone … the big, wide world … it's hers for the taking…"

"Hers? Hers whose?" asked Ivo. "What are you saying about, Stitch Head?"

"Arabella," he replied, tears welling up in his eyes as he closed the door with a KRUNK. "She's gone. She's—"

CLUNK!

CLANK!

Stitch Head froze as he heard the key turn. A moment later the door began to open.

"Mucky rotten goats! What's the big idea, shutting the door in my face?" said Arabella. She pushed open the door, key in hand, and strode through.

"YaBBit! SWaRTiKi!" yapped Pox. He flitted delightedly on to Arabella's shoulder and began chewing her hair with glee.

"Arabella!" cried Stitch Head. "But I thought—"

"What? That I was going to run off with Dotty Dauntless?" she laughed. "I did think about it. But d'you know what? I like monsters and I like trouble ... and I get both right here. This castle is where *I* belong, too."

"But – but when you ran out of the door," said Stitch Head with a sniff. "I was so sure you were..."

"You soppy sewn-up so-and-so ... I went after Dotty for *you*," said Arabella, giving him a friendly punch on the arm. Stitch Head wiped a tear from his eye ... and noticed Arabella was in her stocking feet.

"What – what happened to your boots?" he asked.

"You know how Dotty can't resist a wager?" she explained. "Well, I bet her there was nothing in the world she could offer me that would make me give up my kicking boots. But it turns out I was wrong ... I lost the bet."

Arabella pulled a crumpled piece of paper out of her pocket. It was the deeds to Castle Grotteskew.

"I don't understand," Stitch Head muttered. "Why – why do you have the deeds?"

"Dotty offered me the deeds in a straight swap for my boots," she said with a wink. "To be honest, I reckon she knew I was playing her … I reckon she wanted to do the right thing."

"The right thing?" repeated a baffled Stitch Head.

"The way I see it, if anyone should own this place, it ain't Dotty Dauntless, and it definitely ain't mad old Professor Erasmus … it's you," explained Arabella. She pressed the deeds into Stitch Head's hand. "Reckon Dotty must have agreed with me, too, 'cause she signed the deeds over to you."

"T-to me?" Stitch Head stuttered.

"It's *yours*, Stitch Head," said Arabella. "Castle Grotteskew is yours now."

Stitch Head stared at the piece of paper, his mouth agape. He had never owned anything, never mind a castle. He wasn't sure what to think, or what to say. In the end he just muttered, "Thank you."

"Did I hear what you are saying? Stitch Head owns us now?" asked Ivo, as he and the Creature joined them.

"GRuKK!" protested Pox.

"No ... no one owns anyone," Stitch Head assured them. He looked at Arabella and a smile spread across his patchwork face.

"You can't own a life … or an almost-life."

"NEVER mind that, LOOK!" boomed the Creature, pointing with all three arms at Arabella's feet. "ARABELLA'S got no BOOTS! THAT means she can't KICK us any more!"

"You reckon so, d'you?" replied Arabella with a chuckle. "I don't need no blinkin' boots for kicking you lot! Come 'ere!"

With that, Arabella started chasing the Creature and Ivo around the courtyard as they laughed and squealed.

Stitch Head smiled again, and peered up at the stars. Then he closed the Great Door — *his* door — and felt more at home than ever.

Have you read...

In CASTLE GROTTESKEW
something BIG
is about to happen...
...to someone SMALL.

Join a mad professor's forgotten
creation as he steps out of the
shadows into the adventure
of an almost-lifetime...

In CASTLE GROTTESKEW

Someone SMALL
is about to set sail
on a BIG adventure.

Join a mad professor's forgotten
creation as he prepares for an
almost-life on the high seas...

In CASTLE GROTTESKEW
Someone SMALL
is about to get
into BIG trouble.

Join a mad professor's
forgotten creation as he gets
caught up in a web of mystery…

In CASTLE
GROTTESKEW
Someone SMALL
is about to discover
a BIG secret.

Join a mad professor's
forgotten creation as he fights
for his heart and soul…

Someone
SMALL
is about to
end up in a
a BIG stew.

Join a mad professor's
forgotten creation as his appetite
for adventure is tested
to the limit…

VISIT THE AUTHOR'S WEBSITE AT:

www.guybass.com

STRIPES PUBLISHING
An imprint of Little Tiger Press
1 The Coda Centre, 189 Munster Road,
London SW6 6AW

A paperback original
First published in Great Britain in 2016

Text copyright © Guy Bass, 2016
Illustrations copyright © Pete Williamson, 2016

ISBN: 978-1-84715-649-5

A CIP catalogue record for this book is
available from the British Library.

Printed and bound in the UK.

2 4 6 8 10 9 7 5 3 1